She wasn't sure exactly what kind of man she'd expected Evan Graham to be.

Hannah had known he wasn't a fool when she'd talked to him on the phone. She wouldn't have invited him out to the house for an interview if she had. Mostly she thought he'd be a little older, and maybe just a little softer and wearier around the edges.

But the man now pausing on the porch seemed not only much too vibrant, but also much too accomplished to be truly interested in the type of work she had to offer him.

She was a thirty-two-year-old widow with a five-year-old son, looking to hire a gardener-slash-handyman to help out on her property, not hoping to snag a boyfriend.

But she couldn't deny the sight of Evan Graham had awakened *something* in her.

Dear Reader,

June, the ideal month for weddings, is the perfect time to celebrate true love. And we are doing it in style here at Silhouette Special Edition as we celebrate the conclusion of several wonderful series. With *For the Love of Pete*, Sherryl Woods happily marries off the last of her ROSE COTTAGE SISTERS. It's Jo's turn this time— and she'd thought she'd gotten Pete Catlett out of her system for good. But at her childhood haven, anything can happen! Next, MONTANA MAVERICKS: GOLD RUSH GROOMS concludes with Cheryl St.John's *Million-Dollar Makeover*. We finally learn the identity of the true heir to the Queen of Hearts Mine—and no one is more shocked than the owner herself, the plain-Jane town… dog walker. When she finds herself in need of financial advice, she consults devastatingly handsome Riley Douglas—but she soon finds his influence exceeds the business sphere.…

And speaking of conclusions, Judy Duarte finishes off her BAYSIDE BACHELORS miniseries with *The Matchmakers' Daddy*, in which a wrongly imprisoned ex-con finds all kinds of second chances with a beautiful single mother and her adorable little girls. Next up in GOING HOME, Christine Flynn's heartwarming miniseries, is *The Sugar House*, in which a man who comes home to right a wrong finds himself falling for the woman who's always seen him as her adversary. Patricia McLinn's next book in her SOMETHING OLD, SOMETHING NEW… miniseries, *Baby Blues and Wedding Bells*, tells the story of a man who suddenly learns that his niece is really…his daughter. And in *The Secrets Between Them* by Nikki Benjamin, a divorced woman who's falling hard for her gardener learns that he is in reality an investigator hired by her ex-father-in-law to try to prove her an unfit mother.

So enjoy all those beautiful weddings, and be sure to come back next month! Here's hoping you catch the bouquet.…

Gail Chasan
Senior Editor

Please address questions and book requests to:
Silhouette Reader Service
U.S.: 3010 Walden Ave., P.O. Box 1325, Buffalo, NY 14269
Canadian: P.O. Box 609, Fort Erie, Ont. L2A 5X3

The Secrets Between Them

NIKKI BENJAMIN

SPECIAL EDITION®

Published by Silhouette Books

America's Publisher of Contemporary Romance

 SILHOUETTE BOOKS

ISBN 0-373-24692-7

THE SECRETS BETWEEN THEM

This edition published by arrangement with Harlequin Books S.A.

® and TM are trademarks of Harlequin Books S.A., used under license.
Trademarks indicated with ® are registered in the United States Patent
and Trademark Office, the Canadian Trade Marks Office and in other
countries.

Visit Silhouette Books at www.eHarlequin.com

Printed in U.S.A.

Books by Nikki Benjamin

Silhouette Special Edition

Emily's House #539
On the Whispering Wind #663
The Best Medicine #716
It Must Have Been the Mistletoe #782
My Baby, Your Child #880
Only St. Nick Knew #928
The Surprise Baby #1189
The Major and the Librarian #1228
Expectant Bride-To-Be #1368
Rookie Cop #1444
Loving Leah #1526
Prince of the City #1575
The Baby They Both Loved #1635
The Secrets Between Them #1692

Silhouette Intimate Moments

A Man To Believe In #359
Restless Wind #519
The Wedding Venture #645
The Lady and Alex Payton #729
Daddy by Default #789

NIKKI BENJAMIN

was born and raised in the Midwest, but after years in the Houston area, she considers herself a true Texan. Nikki says she's always been an avid reader. (Her earliest literary heroines were Nancy Drew, Trixie Belden and Beany Malone.) Her writing experience was limited, however, until a friend started penning a novel and encouraged Nikki to do the same. One scene led to another, and soon she was hooked.

For Bert, Geri and Jill Church with deepest appreciation
for welcoming me so warmly into your
lovely Appalachian mountain home.
Special thanks, as well, to Geri and my son, Nick,
for all of your help with Hannah's garden.

Chapter One

Hannah James heard the crunch of tires on the long, winding, gravel drive that connected her beloved North Carolina mountain home to the longer, even more winding road to Boone with an odd mixture of emotions. Certainly uppermost was a sense of relief.

The man with the pleasant voice who had called an hour earlier in response to her ad in the local paper had obviously followed through with his promise. He had come, as she'd hoped he would, to meet with her in person to discuss more fully the job she had on offer.

But a small measure of apprehension also made Hannah's stomach flutter. Not all that long ago—almost a year to be exact—she had sworn that she would never allow another man into her life, much less onto her property.

Unfortunately, she had made that vow without taking into account the amount of work necessary to transform the run-down greenhouses and overgrown gardens into the kind of thriving business that had once provided her parents with a source of income. Nor had she fully acknowledged just how alone she was in the world following the death of her husband—she and her five-year-old son, Will.

Her parents had died within a few months of each other almost seven years ago, leaving her with no close family until her marriage to Stewart James. She'd had a small circle of friends in Boone, of course, and she'd always been on good terms with her nearby neighbors. But isolated as she'd been during the last two years of Stewart's life, she had gradually lost contact with all of them.

She'd had no one to whom she could turn for help. At least no one to whom she could *comfortably* turn, Hannah amended, remembering the speculative glint she'd seen in Stewart's father's eyes whenever his gaze fixed on Will at the funeral service.

Stewart had thwarted his father's wishes in many small ways over the years, starting long before she had met him. But Randall James had been most incensed by his son's decision to marry someone as plain and as poor as he'd considered Hannah to be. He'd refused to attend their wedding ceremony and had followed through on his threat to cut off Stewart financially. To Stewart's credit, he hadn't minded in the least. He'd said more than once that they were better off estranged from the old man than living under his control.

Randall had chosen to keep his distance even after

Will was born. Though Hannah had sent him a card announcing the arrival of his grandson, he hadn't responded in any way. She hadn't told Stewart about his father's frigid indifference. But she'd remembered it well enough that she hadn't gone to the man for help when Stewart first began to act irrationally. She'd been sure that if the old man acknowledged her at all, it would only be to blame her for his son's violent mood swings—just as she'd blamed herself.

Hannah hadn't been able to justify denying Randall's right to know his son had died, however. Though she might have if she'd known how he'd treat her at the funeral service. He had spoken not a word to her until they were ready to leave the cemetery, but he didn't once take his eyes off Will. Hannah had found his sudden, intense interest frightening, with good reason, as she'd soon discovered.

Grasping her arm roughly, he'd halted her progress to the waiting limousine. In a voice pitched too low to be heard by anyone else, he had quite calmly, yet quite forcefully told her just how much he was willing to pay her to hand over her son to be raised by him in the luxury of his stately home in Asheville.

His proposal had been so insane that Hannah had laughed in his face. In a fit of rage, Randall had accused her of using Stewart all along to gain financially. He even went so far as to say she had probably allowed him to die just so she could collect on his life insurance policy. Then he had questioned her mental stability in such a sinister manner that a chill had crept up her spine—

"Mommy, Mommy, somebody's coming up the drive." Abandoning the tower of wooden blocks he'd been building in the middle of the brightly colored rag rug on the living room floor, Will joined her by the long, wide window that faced east down the gentle slope of the mountain. "Who is it, Mommy? Who is it?" he asked, his high young voice animated with excitement.

Hardly anyone had come to visit them in the past year. To be honest, hardly anyone had come to visit them since Will had been old enough to notice. His enthusiasm at the prospect of their having a guest—any guest, no matter the reason—spoke volumes to Hannah of his obvious need to socialize.

She had been able to justify keeping to herself in the weeks right after Stewart's death, as well as through the long winter months when snow and ice often made travel difficult, even dangerous. But with the onset of spring, Hannah knew that she could, and should, start taking Will on walks to visit their neighbors and making the drive into Boone with him for more than gasoline and groceries.

"I imagine it's the man who called about the ad I put in the paper for someone to help with the gardens," she said as a late-model Jeep slowly rounded the last curve in the drive and came into view.

On the covered porch, sheltered from the drizzly rain, Nellie, the half-grown hound-dog puppy Hannah had adopted in September, scrambled to her feet, claws clicking on wood, and began to woof halfheartedly. Hannah had to admit that she wasn't much of a watchdog. But Nellie had been very good company on a cold winter night, and she also trailed after Will like a mother hen, keeping a close eye on him during his daily ventures outdoors to play.

"I can help with the gardens, Mommy," Will said as he slipped one small hand into hers.

"I know you can, sweetie, and you have, especially with the seedlings we started in the greenhouse. But there's a lot more work to do than I expected, a lot more than we can do on our own. We're not going to be able to get all the gardens planted as soon as we should without some extra help. You know I put an ad in the paper a couple of weeks ago."

"Yes, I know."

"And I told you that a man called about the ad a little while ago, didn't I?"

"Yes, Mommy. But is he a *nice* man?"

Will's grip on her hand tightened perceptibly as he looked up at her with wide, anxious eyes.

"He sounded nice on the phone," Hannah answered, attempting to reassure not only her son, but herself, as well.

She knew she was taking a chance by allowing a stranger onto her property. She wasn't being totally irresponsible, though. She had talked to the owner of the small motel outside Boone where the man had claimed to be staying, and had been reassured that he wasn't a transient. In fact, he checked into the motel several days ago and he'd paid for his room with a classy credit card.

The Jeep pulled to a stop a few feet from the stone path leading to the porch steps and a moment later the driver's side door swung open.

"Do you know his name?" Will asked.

"Evan Graham."

"Like graham crackers," Will stated with a smile. "I like graham crackers, Mommy."

"I know. So do I."

"He *looks* nice, doesn't he?"

"Very nice," Hannah acknowledged, an unfamiliar curl of sexual awareness tightening in her belly.

Evan Graham strode confidently around the hood of the Jeep and up the walkway to the porch steps, hurrying just a bit to avoid the rain. He was of medium height, maybe five-ten at the most, which still gave him several inches over her shorter stature. He was neatly dressed in a red plaid flannel shirt, sleeves rolled a couple of turns to reveal his muscular forearms, faded jeans that fit his slender build to perfection and brown leather work boots that appeared to be almost new. His thick, straight, golden blond hair was neatly trimmed and his angular jaw clean-shaven.

Hannah knew that appearances could be deceiving, but he didn't seem the least bit threatening as he climbed the porch steps, head down, his tread amazingly light on the well-worn wood. Then he looked up at the house, his gaze shifting slowly left to right. Intelligence evident in the assessing slant of his bright blue eyes, he took obvious note of her and Will standing by the window, acknowledging their presence with a nod and a smile.

Another flutter of apprehension had Hannah's stomach turning somersaults all over again. She wasn't sure exactly what kind of man she'd expected Evan Graham to be.

She had known he wasn't a fool when she'd talked to him on the phone. She wouldn't have invited him out to the house for an interview if he was. Mostly she'd thought he'd be older—closer to fifty rather than forty—and maybe just a little softer and a little wearier around the edges.

But the man now pausing on the porch to rub Nellie's long, silky ears as the dog wriggled up against him encouragingly seemed not only much too vibrant, but also much too accomplished to be truly interested in the type of work she had to offer him.

"Nellie likes him," Will said.

"Nellie likes just about everybody," Hannah reminded her son, smiling at him as she gave his hand a squeeze.

"Are you going to ask him to come inside the house?"

"That *would* be a good idea, wouldn't it?"

Prompted by her son's reminder of good manners, Hannah moved away from the window at last. Having seen her standing there, the man already knew that she was aware of his arrival. There seemed to be no need for her to wait until he knocked on the door.

She smoothed a hand over the wisps of hair that had come loose from her braid as she reached for the knob, and wished for the first time in months that cosmetics were a part of her daily routine.

In the next instant, however, Hannah chided herself for being silly. She was a thirty-two-year-old widow with a five-year-old son looking to hire a gardener-slash-handyman to help out on her property, not hoping to snag a boyfriend. But she couldn't deny that the sight of Evan Graham *had* awakened *something* in her—*something* that made it all the more disappointing that he would likely turn down the job. Once he had an idea of exactly what it would involve—hard work—and what it wouldn't—a decent wage—she knew he'd be long gone.

"Mr. Graham?" she asked as she opened the door wide, her tone cool but polite.

"Evan...Evan Graham." He gave Nellie one last pat on her head, then straightened so that his eyes met hers, again with a shrewdness that gave her pause. Extending his hand, he added with equal formality, "And you're Mrs. James?"

"Hannah James," she replied, pleased by the firmness of his handshake, but also relieved that he kept it brief, and eminently impersonal.

"I'm Will," her son announced, squeezing next to her in the doorway, his dark-eyed gaze eager and inquisitive. "And that's Nellie, the dog."

"Well, hello, Will. It's very nice to meet you." As Will giggled with delight, Evan Graham turned in Nellie's direction and made a formal bow. "And hello to you, too, Nellie, the dog."

"She forgot that she's not supposed to chew on the corner of the living room rug again, so she's having a time-out on the porch."

"Yes, she most certainly is," Hannah agreed with another smile for her son. Then she glanced at Evan Graham again and noted a similar softening of his expression as he, too, eyed Will with kindly interest. Reassured in a way she couldn't quite explain, she stepped back and gestured invitingly. "Why don't you come inside the house, Mr. Graham. It's much warmer in the kitchen than it is on the porch, and I've just made a fresh pot of coffee."

"Sounds good to me," he replied with an appreciative smile genuine enough to chase some of the iciness from his eyes.

"Can Nellie come inside the house, too? Please, can she?" Will pleaded. "I'll play with her in the living room while you talk to Mr. Graham and I promise, promise, *promise* not to let her chew on the rug again."

Nellie gazed at Hannah contritely with her soulful brown eyes, as if aware that her fate hung in the balance.

"All right," Hannah agreed, sure that she was giving in much too easily when Nellie scrambled past her without a backward glance, ears flapping and nails clicking on the wood floor, Will galloping after her, futilely calling her name.

"Sometimes I wonder who's really in charge around here," Hannah admitted in a rueful tone.

"You seem to have things pretty well under control," Evan said, stepping past her into the house, then pausing to survey his surroundings as she closed the door.

Hannah couldn't be sure, but she thought she detected the faintest hint of surprise in his voice. She wondered what he had expected to find there as she, too, eyed the neat and tidy interior of her home.

The door to the porch opened directly into the L-shaped living room, dining room and kitchen area. The rooms were all simply furnished with a mixture of recently dusted and polished antique rosewood and mahogany furniture and a more contemporary, comfortably upholstered grouping of sofa, loveseat, chair and ottoman.

Some of Will's toys were scattered about on the rag rug, and some of her books and gardening magazines were handily stacked on an end table. But there was no real mess in evidence—never had been.

"I learned a long time ago that it takes a lot less energy to keep up with the housework on a daily basis than to let everything go and then have to deal with the upheaval. Unfortunately, I wasn't able to apply the same effort to my greenhouses and gardens during my husband's illness. Now I need help getting the beds cleaned out and the seedlings in the ground so I'll have plants and produce to sell at the market this summer."

"That's why I'm here," Evan said.

He followed her lead into the kitchen area and paused by the round wooden table, eyeing her expectantly.

"Yes, well…weeding beds, turning compost into the soil and dividing perennials for replanting is hard, physical labor, and moving dozens of seedlings from their little pots to garden plots can be tedious. I can't afford to pay you much, either," Hannah advised, considering it best to be completely honest with him at the outset.

"I understand," he stated simply.

Turning to take mugs from a cabinet, Hannah was tempted to ask him how he could possibly understand anything about her life when she often found it hard to do herself. Evan Graham didn't seem the type to let such a question pass, though, and she wasn't prepared to discuss with a virtual stranger those aspects of her recent past that were better kept to herself.

"Are you still interested in the job, then?" she asked as she glanced over her shoulder at him.

"I wouldn't be here otherwise."

He met her gaze and smiled, seeming perfectly at ease in her small kitchen. Her heart fluttered as she realized that he almost seemed to belong there, too.

"In that case, have a seat and we'll talk some more." With a small indrawn breath, Hannah turned away again, reached for the carafe full of hot, fresh coffee and filled both mugs.

"Cream or sugar?"

"Cream if you have it, please."

"I do, but it's the real thing. I have skim milk, too, if you'd rather have that."

Holding both mugs in one hand, Hannah took spoons from a drawer and napkins from a basket on the counter with the other then carried the lot to the table.

"I'll have the cream," he said as she crossed to the refrigerator. "Indulgent as it is."

"It's a small splurge, all things considered, or so I like to tell myself," Hannah admitted with a smile.

She retrieved the carton of cream from the refrigerator and set it on the table. Then she went over to the pantry and took the tin can of chocolate chip cookies that she'd baked yesterday afternoon off the shelf.

"Mmm, those look good," Evan said as Hannah set the can of cookies on the table. "Another small splurge?"

The corners of his eyes crinkled as he favored her with a teasing smile.

"Only if you eat just one. More than that and you'll be well on your way to intemperance," Hannah cautioned in a playful tone—shocked that she was actually flirting with this man.

"And intemperance would be a bad thing?" he countered, bantering back easily.

"Not necessarily."

Returning Evan's smile ruefully, Hannah sat across from him, then looked away as she added cream to her coffee and chose a cookie from the can. She sensed his gaze on her, watchful and alert, but instinctively she sensed as well that he meant her and Will no harm. In fact, she felt quite comfortable, sitting with him in her warm, cozy kitchen, sheltered as they were from the cool, gray, rainy day.

He didn't loom large and threatening in any way. Rather, he sat back in his chair, his posture loose, lazily stirring his coffee with the spoon he held in one long-fingered, masculine hand.

Had he cloaked himself in a brilliant disguise in order to gain entry to her home to commit some dastardly deed, she was sure that deed would have been done and he would have already been long gone.

"I have a feeling you're rarely intemperate, Mrs. James," Evan said, setting his spoon on a napkin, then helping himself to one of her cookies.

"Call me Hannah, please," she insisted, then added after a moment's thought, "And you're right—I'm not really the intemperate type. What about you, Mr. Graham?"

"Evan, please, and no, I don't tend to be intemperate, either, although I'm definitely having another one of these cookies. They're delicious."

"Thanks."

Hannah smiled graciously, inwardly pleased with his praise. Then she shifted her gaze back to his hands again. She had expected them to be work-roughened, but they were unmarked by either scars or calluses. His nails were clean and neatly trimmed, as well, not soil-stained or ragged.

"You're looking rather pensive all of a sudden," he said, startling her just a little with the depth of his perception.

Though, to be honest, she had never been all that

good at hiding her thoughts, more often than not causing herself a great deal of embarrassment as a result. She didn't blush or stammer now, however. Her concern was completely legitimate.

"You're not used to working with your hands, are you?" she asked, meeting his gaze.

For a moment, he looked startled, then smiled sheepishly.

"It's that obvious?"

"Yes, it is."

She touched a finger to the back of her hand for just a moment by way of explanation.

"I haven't done much gardening lately, or any other type of manual labor," he admitted. "But that doesn't mean I have a problem with it."

"What *have* you been doing lately…Evan?" Hannah asked, giving in to her growing curiosity about him.

"Working for a computer software company in Charlotte that was bought out by a larger company. I was downsized out the door with a moderate compensation package about a month ago." He reached into the pocket of his plaid flannel shirt and pulled out a neatly folded square of paper. "I have a list of references, personal and professional. You're more than welcome to call them."

Hannah took the square of paper from him, unfolded it and glanced at the names, addresses and telephone numbers neatly typed on it. Not that the list alone offered verification—she didn't recognize any of the names on it. Still, the offer of references that she could call added to her inclination to trust in him.

Yet she couldn't help continuing to wonder why

he'd chosen to leave the city—not to mention give up the possibility of securing another lucrative white-collar job in computer technology—to work as a low-paid gardener and handyman on a farm in the mountains of North Carolina.

"So what brings you here, of all places?"

She met his gaze again, making no effort to hide her puzzlement.

"I've been wanting a change of pace and a change of place the past couple of years. Being downsized has given me the opportunity to make those changes. I'd really like to find out if I'm any happier working at a different kind of job in a different kind of place than I was putting in twelve- and fourteen-hour days in an office in Charlotte," he replied without hesitation.

"But you won't be making nearly as much money working for me," Hannah pointed out.

"I don't need a lot of money right now. I do, however, need a place to live in the area, at least temporarily, and your ad did say room and board was included."

"I *can* offer you that," Hannah agreed. "You'd have the room on the second floor all to yourself. It's furnished, of course, and there's a bathroom with a shower stall up there, too. It was my room when I was growing up, then my husband used it as his study after Will was born so we could put Will in the spare bedroom downstairs. I can also provide three meals a day as part of the package."

"Having sampled your chocolate chip cookies, I'd say that sounds very good to me."

He shot a wry grin her way as he took a third cookie from the can on the table.

"I *am* a pretty good cook," Hannah admitted, allowing the slightest hint of pride to edge her words as she smiled, too.

"I'd like to sign on with you, then, Hannah...if you'll have me."

"I appreciate your interest, but in all fairness I really should take you for a walk around the property first so you'll know exactly what you have ahead of you. Do you have any rain gear with you?"

"A jacket in the Jeep. I'll get it and meet you on the porch, okay?"

"Sounds good to me," Hannah replied as she pushed away from the table and stood.

Evan stood, as well, picked up his mug and carried it to the sink, then started toward the door. Hannah put the lid on the cookie tin, then followed after him to collect her own rain jacket from the row of pegs on the wall.

"Can me and Nellie go with you, too?" Will asked as he scrambled to his feet along with the dog, his blocks forgotten.

"Nellie and I," Hannah corrected gently. "And yes, you can go with us. But first get a towel from the bathroom cabinet to dry Nellie when we're ready to come inside again."

"Okay."

As Will scampered off, Nellie galloping after him, Hannah turned back to Evan. She saw him watching her son, his gaze intent. The vaguely bemused look in his eyes gave her pause all over again.

Was he as honest and as decent as she wanted to believe he was? Or was he hiding something unsavory about himself and his reason for being there behind a careful facade meant to give her a false sense of security?

"Is something wrong?" she asked him, her voice wavering with sudden uncertainly.

Immediately, Evan Graham focused his attention on her once again, his expression shifting smoothly, softening in the merest blink of an eye.

"Not at all, Mrs. James. I was just thinking how lucky you are to have such a happy, healthy son."

His friendly, open manner made it easy to shake off her doubts about him. Too easy, perhaps, but the condition of her greenhouses and gardens had turned her into a beggar who couldn't afford to be a chooser. She wanted—needed—him to check out okay for the sake of her business. It didn't have anything to do with the way his presence made her feel.

"Yes, I'm very lucky to have such a happy, healthy son," she said.

Evan Graham nodded once, seeming to confirm something in his own mind. Then he opened the door and stepped out onto the porch.

"Guess I'd better get my jacket so you can give me the grand tour."

"You'll get wet otherwise."

"I wouldn't want that to happen," he said, closing the door behind him.

Hannah took her jacket from the peg, but made no immediate move to put it on. Instead she lurked by the window, watching as Evan Graham ambled down the walkway to his Jeep. He was an interesting and an attractive man in a lot of ways—probably too attractive to her under the circumstances, she acknowledged with a grim twist of her lips.

He was still a stranger, after all. Anyone could adopt a polite, conscientious, ingratiating manner for the short time necessary to get a foot in the door of a trusting woman. How he behaved toward her, and toward Will, on a day-to-day basis would reveal much more about the true nature of his character.

In the meantime, however, there was no harm in being glad that he seemed to want to work with her. After all the months of hurt and fear and loneliness she'd endured, she realized she was as much in need of companionship as any other living, breathing human being would have been. And she couldn't see any harm in *cautiously* enjoying Evan Graham's company.

"We're ready," Will announced, joining her by the window.

He'd put on his rain jacket and had a towel clutched in his arms. Beside him, Nellie wriggled excitedly.

"Let's go then," Hannah said as she moved away from the window.

Slipping into her jacket, as well, she savored for a long moment the sense of an adventure about to begin—small, and perhaps silly, as it might be.

Chapter Two

Evan took his rain jacket from the backseat of the Jeep and put in on slowly, giving himself a little time to organize his thoughts. Not an easy task, he admitted, considering his current state of confusion.

He had rarely been as disconcerted by anyone's appearance or behavior as he'd been by that of Hannah James. She hadn't been anything like the kind of woman Randall James had described to him less than a week ago. With her long, dark hair pulled back in a single, simple, neatly twined braid and not an ounce of makeup on her face, there had been no outer artifice about her at all. And although the jeans, red sweater and low-heeled, ankle-high boots she wore hadn't been new, they were most certainly neat and clean.

Nor had Hannah acted in any way like the evil, avaricious and unfeeling person her former father-in-law had accused her of being. For someone who had supposedly allowed her husband to die in order to collect money from his life insurance policy, she seemed to live a very simple, very quiet life.

Either Hannah James had magically transformed herself into a warm, kind, honest, loving mother, her home into a serene and orderly haven and her son into a normal, happy, healthy five-year-old, or his client had lied to him point-blank.

Years of working as a police officer and then as a private investigator had honed Evan's ability to read people. He was successful enough to choose his clients, and he did so based largely on his belief that they were being honest with him.

He rarely missed the signs that someone was lying to him. In fact, he couldn't recall one time that he'd taken on a new client only to discover that he'd been grossly and very likely intentionally misled.

Granted, there were always two sides to any story. People seldom viewed the same situation in exactly the same way, and when the people involved were also adversaries, there was an even greater chance of disparity between them. Evan had learned that accusations could sometimes be wrapped in exaggeration.

A lonely, insecure wife would paint her friendly, mildly flirtatious, desperate-to-meet-a-deadline-at-the-office husband as a carousing ladies' man who cheated on her regularly. The owner of a small company, upon seeing an occasionally rabble-rousing employee driving an expensive new car, would assume the employee was stealing from him in some way.

Or a wealthy man who had recently lost his only son would insist without the slightest hesitation that his grandson's life was being endangered by a scheming, psychotic mother who insisted on forcing the child to live in poverty, isolation and quite possibly even degradation.

Evan had talked to Randall James first by telephone and then face-to-face when he had met with the man at his office in Charlotte. Evan had asked questions and Randall had answered in a seemingly forthright manner, his gaze direct, hands resting quietly on the arms of his chair. Not once had he resorted to histrionics. Yet Randall's concern had been more than evident, and understandable, as well, to Evan.

Quite understandable, in fact, considering the kind of childhood he'd had, living in debilitating poverty in the so-called care of a mother who had been anything but loving and protective, especially when she was busy drinking herself into oblivion. Rescuing children from similar circumstances involving parental abuse had been a top priority of Evan's for many years.

But Hannah and her son weren't living in debilitating poverty. Her home was warm and inviting, as well as sturdy and secure, not some run-down shack barely providing a roof over her head. He wondered if Randall James had ever actually been there, then decided he couldn't possibly have been and still describe the place in such a derogatory way.

Nor had Evan been able to detect the slightest sign of either scheming or psychosis in Hannah James. She had seemed a little shy, but in an endearing kind of way. And she'd been wary of him, of course, as any woman living on her own with any sense at all would be wary of a strange man, no matter how presentable he appeared to be.

She would have to take some chances in order to find the help she needed, though. That she seemed interested in taking a chance on him certainly worked in his favor.

But if Randall James had lied to him about Hannah, was there really any need for him to sign on with her in the guise of hired help?

Evan still found it hard to believe that he had been fooled so completely by the man. Had his usually sharp and savvy instincts taken a temporary powder during his meeting with Randall James? Or was Hannah James a highly skilled actress, masterfully hiding her conniving and her craziness behind a mask of normalcy edged with sweetness and light?

It would take a huge amount of talent to pull off such a performance for more than a few days—a week at the most. Though why she would feel the need to impress the likes of him Evan couldn't say. She knew him only as a man in search of a job and a place to live. And forcing a five-year-old child to appear happy when he wasn't had to be almost impossible to do.

Seeing Hannah, Will and Nellie the dog step out of the house onto the porch, Evan hesitated a moment longer, eyeing the threesome thoughtfully, trying to decide whether to stay or to go. When Hannah caught sight of him, raised her hand and waved to him, he finished fastening the snaps down the front of his jacket, his decision finally made.

He could see no immediate harm in investigating Hannah James a little further. She *had* been living with the boy in relative isolation, not only according

to Randall, but also according to the few people he'd
managed to question in Boone, and that *did* cause
Evan some concern. There was also the fact that she
wouldn't be able to hide her true nature from him for
long, living in the house with her, as he'd be. It
wouldn't cost him anything except a week of his time,
and Randall James was paying him quite handsomely
for that already.

Though Evan wasn't choosing to continue his cha-
rade awhile longer out of any sense of duty to the man.
Instead he felt a responsibility toward young Will to
determine whether he really was a happy, healthy
child, safe and secure in his widowed mother's care.

Pulling up the hood of his jacket to fend off the
heavy mist in the mountain air as Hannah and Will had
done, Evan joined them at the foot of the porch steps.
Nellie wriggled up to him, poked her cold nose into the
palm of his hand, snuffled a moment, then loped off
along an overgrown stone path that led around the far
side of the house. Will took off after her, as well, calling her name to no apparent good.

"It's pretty wet out here, and muddy, too. Are you
sure you want to risk ruining your new boots?" Hannah asked, peering up at him from under the brim of
the dark green hood framing her face.

The hesitation Evan heard in her voice coupled with
the concern that shadowed her soft brown eyes reminded him anew of how the real Hannah James didn't
jibe with the Hannah James he'd expected to find there.
She was considerate almost to a fault, and in a way that
spoke to him of caution. It was almost as if she were
trying to guess at what might upset or annoy him so as
to avoid having it happen.

"They're meant to be work boots and I was told they're waterproof. Might as well put them to the test," he replied.

"All right, then," she said with obvious relief. "Let's start with the greenhouses."

As Hannah turned and headed down the stone path, Evan realized how easily and how naturally she blended into the lush spring landscape. She moved with grace and confidence, head up and shoulders squared, leading him wordlessly into her world. He followed after her with a willingness that had more to do with her womanly allure than his real reason for being there.

Evan had already noted the sturdiness of her cedar-plank house. He had also seen that although her property was situated on the gentle slope of a heavily wooded mountain, the area around the house had been neatly carved into a series of clearings. These clearings led in terraced steps from the main road to the house, then on past the house for a good way before running, once again, into dense forest growth.

Years of hard work had obviously gone into creating this quiet, peaceful place that seemed to him like a hidden jewel. But the neglect Hannah had mentioned was obvious, as well. Barely able to discern the borders of various beds almost hidden by an odd mix of dead-fall and new vegetation now running rampant, Evan understood immediately just how desperate she had to be for help.

"It's really gotten away from me," she said, gesturing all around her with one hand as she glanced back at him. "But I guess you can see that for yourself."

"Everything looks very green and lush to me. But

I admit I'm not much good at telling weeds from whatever's worth cultivating," Evan replied.

"There *are* perennials coming up under all the stuff that died off over the winter, but there are lots of weeds, too. We'll have to clear out the dead stuff first, of course, then get rid of the weeds, divide the perennials for replanting as necessary and turn compost into the soil."

She gestured again at a large, square, wooden box about four feet tall that Evan assumed held her compost heap.

"The vegetable gardens and apple trees are on the slope down from the house," she continued. "I've pruned the trees already, but the vegetable gardens have to be cleared and composted, as well. Then we'll have to plant the seedlings I've started in the greenhouses."

"Sounds like you've done a lot of work already," Evan acknowledged.

"Actually, I've barely scratched the surface," Hannah admitted with another glance over her shoulder, concern still evident in her eyes. "The really hard work is yet to be done."

"I've never minded hard work," Evan said, wanting to reassure her.

Too late he realized that he was actually leading her on. He was only there to find out if she was endangering her son in any way, and he wouldn't likely need more than a week to make that determination. Then he would return to his office in Charlotte, write up a report for Randall James, collect the remainder of his fee and immediately get busy on another case.

He would only be able to help Hannah make a small

dent in all the work that needed to be done before he left
her on her own again. The thought didn't sit well with
him.

"I'm so glad to hear that," Hannah said.

Once again, her tone held more than a hint of relief,
causing Evan to suffer another irksome twinge of conscience. He could try to justify his reasons for deceiving Hannah James, but bottom line, he knew that at the
very least he was going to willfully become a source
of grave disappointment to her.

Such a probability left him feeling oddly ashamed
and apologetic. Still, he had a job to do—one that involved the well-being of a five-year-old child. For
Evan, the good of the boy had to come first. Hannah
could take care of herself; Will couldn't.

As they rounded the house, Evan saw the object of
his concern waiting patiently for them, along with Nellie, by the door of one of two small, old-fashioned,
glass-windowed greenhouses a few yards ahead. He
had expected them to be larger, longer and lower like
the commercial greenhouses used by wholesale nurs-
eries. Hannah's were much more picturesque, adding
to the landscape in a most charming way.

The buildings sat side by side just beyond the
wide, wood-plank deck built onto the back of the
house. Not one of the panes of glass was broken, and
all appeared to have been recently washed, allowing
a clear view of the long tables filled with small pots
within the walls. Vents with fans had also been in-
stalled to help with temperature control during the
summer months that could be surprisingly warm even
in the mountains. Despite the tall trees surrounding
the area at a good distance, on a sunny day the green-

houses would get the full benefit of several hours of bright sunlight.

"Can I go in the greenhouse, Mommy, and check on our seedlings?" Will asked.

"Let me grab Nellie first," Hannah replied.

Joining her son by the door, she wrapped a hand around the dog's collar and held her back as Will slipped into the greenhouse.

"We made the mistake of taking her in the green-houses with us when she was a puppy. Now she's like a bull in a china shop," Hannah explained. "She doesn't mean to be, but she gets so excited that she wriggles and wags her tail and ends up knocking over a whole shelf of little peat pots before we can stop her."

"Poor girl," Evan said, reaching out to scratch the dog's floppy ears. "You're just too happy for your own good, aren't you?"

Nellie gazed up at him and offered a woof in seem-ing agreement, making Hannah smile along with him.

She urged him to go into the greenhouse, then to the dog she ordered sternly, "Sit, Nellie and *stay*," and followed after him.

Though the greenhouse wasn't very large at all, the interior was laid out in a surprisingly spacious way. The air was warmer inside than outside the glass walls, but the humidity wasn't as dense as Evan had expected, and smelled of rich, dark soil and green, leafy things.

The rows of tables were chock-full of little pots and trays filled with small, yet obviously healthy plants, all of which looked about the same to him. Will had no trouble telling one from another, though. Standing by the table against the south-facing wall of windows, he pointed here and there with excitement and delight.

"Look, Mommy, look, Mr. Graham—the tomatoes are really starting to grow now. So are the green peppers and the lettuce and the cucumbers and the squash. We're going to have to start moving them out to the beds really soon."

"I know," Hannah agreed, then to Evan she added, "We'll have to start clearing out the vegetable gardens as soon as the rain lets up—hopefully tomorrow if the latest weather forecast can be trusted. We're also going to have to move the seedlings outside to get them hardened off for life in the beds."

"Hardened off?" Evan eyed her quizzically.

"Seedlings started in a greenhouse are sheltered from the wind, strong sun and varying temperatures. They need to develop tougher tissues gradually before they're planted in the ground. Otherwise they don't grow and produce as well as they should."

"I see," Evan said. "I also see that there is a lot more to gardening than I ever imagined."

"You have no idea." Hannah rolled her eyes, then met his gaze, her smile questing. "I hope I'm not scaring you off."

"Not at all. But..."

Evan hesitated, trying to decide how best to word the questions that had sprung to mind as he'd realized just how labor-intensive it was to grow fruits, vegetables and flowers to sell at the local market. He didn't want to offend Hannah by appearing to doubt the wisdom of trying to support herself and her son in such a way. Nor did he want to make her unduly suspicious of him by seeming overly interested in her financial situation.

"That *but* didn't sound encouraging," she prompted

after a long moment, her smile fading. "Especially since you haven't even seen the vegetable gardens yet."

"Not to worry. I'm still interested in the job," he assured her. "I was just wondering if the return is worth all the work involved."

"I admit I'll never get rich selling produce at the market in town. But the gardens helped to provide an income for my parents, and I don't need a lot of money to get by. I own several hundred acres of land and the house free and clear, and I have savings set aside from my husband's life insurance policy for Will's education. I've also been thinking about going back to teaching since he'll be starting kindergarten in the fall. In the meantime, it seems a shame not to use the gardens as they were meant to be.

"There isn't much of a financial return, all things considered. But the real return for me is in having a hand in producing things that give me pleasure. If you plan to stick around, you'll see what I mean."

"Sounds to me like it would be a shame if I didn't."

Not an outright lie, but still enough of a prevarication to make Evan look away from her sweet, steady, all-too-hopeful gaze. He wondered why there couldn't be just one thing about Hannah James that he didn't like. Yet at the same time, he was grateful that there wasn't.

"I really should let you reserve judgment until you've seen the vegetable gardens."

"Well, then, let's take a look at them."

With Will and Nellie again leading the way, Evan and Hannah followed another meandering path set with stones around the other side of the house and across the gravel drive. The vegetable gardens were more easily discernible than the flower gardens had been because they were built-up and partitioned off with foot-high wooden frames. But they were just as badly overgrown as the flower beds.

From beyond the clearing in a place hidden by the forest growth came the musical sound of water flowing.

"Do you have a creek back there?" Evan asked.

"It runs from a spring up above the house. There are actually several springs on the property, one of which also serves as our major source of water." Hannah pointed up the slope to where the tree line began. "I have a holding tank up above the house. The water from the spring collects there and then it's piped into the house. I have a water heater, of course, so hot, as well as cold, running water is always available."

"That's good to know." Evan grinned at her, honestly relieved, then turned his attention back to the vegetable gardens, asking, "Do you have any problems with critters getting into the beds?"

"Chicken wire around the beds will keep out the rabbits and the occasional deer that comes to call, and plastic netting keeps out the birds once the little veggies start to appear."

"We can make a scarecrow, too," Will advised, flitting to Hannah's side, then flitting away again, Nellie loping after him. "Just like the one in my favorite storybook."

"A *real* scarecrow?" Evan asked in a teasing tone.

"What can I say? The fun never ends around here." Hannah turned on the path back to the house. "I can show you the upstairs room now, if you'd like."

"I'd like that very much," Evan agreed.

"Come on, Will. Time to go back to the house," she called out to her son.

"Okay, Mommy."

"You said something earlier about pruning your apple trees," Evan said as he walked along the path beside her.

"I have a very small orchard." Hannah waved a hand at a dozen trees, limbs bright with new green leaves, in a clearing farther down the drive. "The trees have bloomed and tiny apples are already starting to grow. We'll have to do some composting down there, too. I also have several walnut trees at the end of the drive. They're big and old and pretty much take care of themselves."

"That's a relief," Evan quipped.

"Oh, it is," Hannah agreed.

Again Evan couldn't help but be taken aback by the sheer amount of physical labor necessary just to prepare for the growing season. He didn't want to even *think* about what must be involved in maintenance once the plants had been set in the beds, because that would also entail thinking about Hannah either having to look for help again or having to do it all alone.

Tramping along with her in the mist, breathing in the clear, cold air, the dancing waters of the creek providing background music, Evan told himself that he was there *only* to confirm Will's safety in his mother's care. Yet he couldn't deny that an odd sense of peace had settled over him.

Years had passed since he'd last spent time enjoying the sights, sounds and smells of the natural world. Cooped up in his office, a rented room or a vehicle, and tied to electronic tools of his trade, his experience of the great outdoors had consisted mainly of viewing it from a window. But that was about to change—at least for a week—and he was looking forward to it with a surprising edge of anticipation.

Leaving Will on the porch to towel off Nellie—a task both boy and dog appeared to enjoy—Hannah and Evan took a moment to dry the soles of their boots on the mat, then headed into the house. At Hannah's invitation, Evan hung his jacket on one of the pegs next to hers, followed her across the living room and up the steep, narrow, creaking flight of wooden steps that led to the second floor of the house.

At the top of the staircase a short hall led to a doorway that opened into a long, spacious room built under the eaves of the slanting roof. One end held a bed piled with pillows in white, lace-edged cases and covered with a patchwork quilt done in muted shades of blue and rose and green. A nightstand beside the bed held a brass lamp and there was also a small dresser with a mirror against the far wall.

At the opposite end of the room sat a chair and ottoman upholstered in blue-and-white striped fabric. A row of built-in bookcases full of books lined part of the wall, and there was also a small rolltop desk and an expensive-looking, black leather desk chair, out of place enough for Evan to conclude that it must have belonged to Hannah's husband.

On the polished wood floor were a couple of blue-and-green rag rugs. Banks of wide windows—sans blinds or curtains of any kind—were set shoulder-high in the three outside walls, as well. They not only let in the meager light of the gray day, but also framed views of the woodland treetops that seemed closer when seen from this snug and tranquil aerie.

"The bathroom is over there," Hannah said, nodding toward a doorway that opened into a small, separate area that held a pedestal-style sink, a toilet and a narrow shower stall.

"It's very nice," Evan said with honest appreciation.

"Private, too. You can come up here anytime you want and no one will disturb you," Hannah advised. "You should be fairly comfortable…."

"I'm sure I'll be *very* comfortable," Evan assured her.

"So…are you still interested?" she asked as she turned to leave the room.

"Yes, I am. I can plan to be here first thing tomorrow morning, if you want to hire me."

"I'm very interested. I'll have to check your references, of course—you understand—but why don't you plan to be here tomorrow morning around eight o'clock?" She paused by the door to the porch, took his jacket from the peg and held it out to him. "I'll call you at the hotel if there's a problem."

"Eight it is, unless I hear from you otherwise," Evan agreed.

He had given her the name and telephone number of the motel where he was staying when he'd talked to her earlier. As he put on his jacket and prepared to leave, he wondered if she would call there later that evening to tell him not to come back.

Evan doubted it, considering how much help she needed with her gardens. Everyone on his list of references would cover for him, as well. While all were valid friends and business associates, they had been advised in advance of who Hannah James was and why she might be calling them. Still, the fact that she wanted to check him out more thoroughly rather than blindly inviting him to stay in her home only fed his doubts about Randall's claims.

"Be careful on the drive back to Boone," she said, opening the door for him.

"I will."

On the porch, Will was playing tug with Nellie. The dog had one end of the soggy towel gripped in her teeth and was growling playfully, her tail wagging a mile a minute.

"I'm just about done, Mommy," the boy said, then shrieked as Nellie pulled the towel out of his hands and took off around the side of the porch. "Come back, Nellie, come back!"

"Looks like I'd better get another towel…or two," Hannah said with a rueful grin, adding to Evan as he walked down the porch steps, "See you tomorrow, then?"

"Unless I hear otherwise," he confirmed, then climbed into the Jeep, fit his key in the ignition and started the engine as Hannah reached through the open doorway, grabbed her jacket and went off after boy and dog.

Evan didn't relish the long journey back to Boone on rain-slick, winding mountain roads. But in a strange way he *needed* to put some distance between himself and Hannah, physically as well as mentally.

Nothing about her appearance or her manner had been intentionally alluring—not that he could deny finding her that way. Nor had he seen any reason to be concerned about leaving her alone with her son. Yet he didn't *want* to leave her, and perversely enough that lack of *want* made the *need* even more imperative.

Hannah James had put him at ease with her gentleness and her warmth, her consideration and concern. She had seemed so genuine, so open and so honest that as he guided the Jeep down the gravel drive, fighting an urge to glance in the rearview mirror, the pangs of conscience he'd suffered earlier hit him again at a deeper, more visceral level.

Evan could justify going ahead with his deception, lying to her for Will's sake for a while longer. But he knew he'd be lying to himself if he said that he was only going back there because of the boy. The real draw was Hannah James, herself.

And there was no place in this assignment for that kind of fascination.

Considering all the lies he had already told her, the only way he *could* spend time with her was to sign on as hired help. He could stay a day, a week, a month, but eventually he would have only two choices—he could abandon her knowing full well how much she needed help, or he could tell her the truth about himself and reveal just how seriously he'd betrayed her trust. Lying to people was a given in his line of work. He had done it before and he would do it again, especially to protect a child. But lying to Hannah James didn't sit easy with him.

From what he knew of her now, he believed she deserved better than that from him. But the only real alternative he had was never going back to her house at all. And that, Evan Graham acknowledged as he turned onto the main road back to Boone, he simply couldn't do.

Chapter Three

Hannah set another tray of peat pots filled with seedlings in the sheltered area on the wood deck that she used for the first stage of hardening off the little plants. Straightening, she tipped her face to the sun, squared her shoulders and stretched to relieve the slight kink in her lower back. The pause also gave her time to realize that she was hungry.

Will and Evan Graham were likely ready for a lunch break, as well, she surmised. They had all been working hard since early that morning, and from the slant of the sun, it had to be at least noon.

Verifying that thought, Will joined her on the deck, set down the tray of seedlings he'd been carrying and eyed her hopefully as he asked, "Do you want me to go inside and make some sandwiches, Mommy?"

"How about if you help *me* make the sandwiches?"

She reached out and gently ruffled a hand through his thick, dark hair.

"Okay."

"Round up Nellie, then go in the house and wash your hands while I let Mr. Graham know we're stopping to eat lunch now."

"Okay, Mommy."

As Will tore off up the hill, calling to the dog snuffling at the edge of the woods, Hannah headed around the house and down the path to the vegetable gardens. There Evan had set to work weeding almost as soon as he'd arrived—promptly at eight o'clock as they'd agreed.

She had been so relieved to hear the sound of his Jeep coming up the gravel drive that morning. Until then, she had still doubted that he would actually take the minimum-wage job she'd offered him. Even despite the fact that he had called her early the previous evening and asked if everything went okay with his references, and if she needed anything from town that he could bring with him when he came.

Hannah had not only been surprised by his request, but also pleased. In her estimation, such thoughtfulness on his part boded well for their working relationship. It also made her feel even better about her decision to hire him.

Although his "…that is, if you still want me for the job…" had come back to haunt her later in the night.

She hadn't given his comment much thought at the time he'd made it, airily dismissing it with her own "of course, I do." But at one o'clock in the morning, unable to sleep, she had gone over their conversation in her mind and had wondered if he'd had doubts of his own, the source of which she'd only been able to guess at.

Or had he been offering her a last chance to back out of the bargain they'd màde?

But then, that hadn't made sense. Not if he wanted and needed a job *and* a place to stay in the area as much as he'd claimed he did.

Of course, he could have just *told* her that in order to get a foot in the door—a possibility she hadn't even entertained in the light of day.

Was there a reason his references wouldn't have checked out? Hannah had thought, eyeing the clock on her nightstand grimly. Not that that had been the case at all. Everyone she spoke to had nothing but glowing things to say about Evan Graham. Besides, why would he have offered her references unless he fully expected all of the people he'd listed to vouch for him in a positive way?

Reminding herself that it was important to trust her instincts—and her instinctive feeling about Evan Graham had been good—Hannah had slept at last, soundly enough to awaken at seven o'clock feeling rested and ready for the day ahead. The sunlight peeping through her window had brightened her spirits, as well. They would be able to make the first small dent in all the work that needed to be done—if Evan arrived as planned.

He had pulled up by the porch at eight o'clock on the dot, causing Nellie to bark and wag excitedly and Will, still in his pajamas, to dance around the living room in glee. He had brought along a bag of bagels, still warm from the oven, and a carton of cream cheese from her favorite deli in Boone, and presented both to her with an engaging smile. He'd also looked well rested and more than ready to start work.

"I brought four cinnamon-raisin, four loaded with everything and four whole wheat," he'd said.

"Mmm, perfect choices," she'd replied, delighted by the rare treat.

Glad that she'd eaten only a *small* bowl of cereal earlier, Hannah had helped herself to a cinnamon-raisin bagel as Evan returned to the Jeep and proceeded to move his few belongings to the room upstairs.

He'd had a large, black duffel bag and a laptop computer in an expensive-looking leather carrying case. One trip up the staircase and he joined her in the kitchen, rubbing his hands together briskly to chase away the slight chill of the early-morning mountain air.

Hannah had noted that he was as neat and clean—and attractive—as he'd been the previous day. He'd obviously showered and shaved before leaving the motel, if the slight dampness of his hair and the subtle drift of spicy aftershave she'd caught were any indication. His faded jeans and navy blue sweatshirt appeared older and much more worn than the jeans and flannel shirt he'd had on yesterday, making them more suitable for the rough, outdoor work he'd be doing in the wet, weed-infested beds. She couldn't help but notice his change of clothes did nothing to temper her feminine response to him, but she pushed the realization aside. Evan was her employee— nothing more.

He had accepted a mug of coffee, but turned down a bagel, saying he'd eaten one on his way to her place. Hannah had savored the last few bites of hers, finished her coffee and sent Will to his room to get dressed.

Then she'd led Evan out to the shed where she stored her shovels, rakes, hoes, wheelbarrow and various other gardening tools along with the bags and boxes of organically approved products she preferred to use to nourish and protect her plants, as well as control pests.

She had found a pair of relatively new, heavy-duty gardening gloves for him—originally bought for Stewart who had rarely used them. She'd loaded the gloves, a shovel and a hoe into the wheelbarrow, then turned to Evan.

"I need you to work on the vegetable gardens first," she'd said as he gripped the handles of the wheelbarrow and guided it out of the shed. "They need to be cleaned out completely. It shouldn't be too hard since the ground is pretty wet from all the rain, but it will be a messy job for the same reason."

"What should I do with the stuff I dig up?" he'd asked, looking back at her as they'd headed down the drive.

"You can load it into the wheelbarrow, then transfer it to the compost bin. It's divided into three sections. The one to the left is empty, so we'll use it to start a new batch."

Hannah had met Evan's gaze, hoping she wasn't overwhelming him with his morning's duties. He'd looked amazingly eager to get to work, and she'd smiled encouragingly as they'd continued down the drive, pausing only when they reached the first of the vegetable beds laid out neatly on the gentle slope.

"Be sure to wear the gloves so you don't get blisters or bug bites on your hands," she'd advised him.

"I will."

"I'll put a jug of ice water on the porch for you, too. You're welcome to take a break anytime you want and help yourself to anything you need. There's coffee in the pot on the counter and iced tea in the refrigerator if you'd prefer something besides water. If you have any questions, I'll be working in the greenhouses, moving the seedlings out to the deck so they can start hardening off. Just give a holler."

"I'll do that, too," he said, parking the wheelbarrow and retrieving the gloves.

"We'll stop for lunch around noon or so."

"Sounds good to me."

He'd pulled on the gloves, picked up the hoe, shot her a smile and immediately set to work.

Hannah hadn't talked to Evan again in the four hours that had passed since then. She had caught an occasional glimpse of him, however, as he'd wheeled one load after another of leaves and weeds to the compost bin. Once she had also gone to check on his progress, albeit at a distance, and had been surprised at how quickly and efficiently he was getting the job done.

Not wanting Evan to catch her spying on him, Hannah had meant only to watch him work a minute or two. But the sight of him breaking up clods of weed-choked soil with the hoe, an industrious look on his face, his movements spare and sure, had arrested her attention completely.

He wasn't a big man, bulked up with overdeveloped muscles, but Hannah could easily see the strength and energy in his wiry build. Though he had claimed that he wasn't used to rough, outdoor work, he hadn't appeared to have any problem taking to it. Of course, he'd only been at it a couple of hours.

Reluctantly slipping away to continue her own work in the greenhouses, Hannah had wondered how enthusiastic Evan would be later in the day, not to mention later in the week—if he even lasted that long. She didn't want to be pessimistic about Evan, but with so much riding on his employment working out, she was scared to get too hopeful. Past experience had taught her the danger of that.

Now walking down the drive again, Hannah saw that Evan had finished clearing one of the four-foot by four-foot beds completely and was almost finished with another. She also saw that he'd stripped off his sweatshirt and was about to pull off his white short-sleeve T-shirt, as well. He caught sight of her, paused and smiled somewhat sheepishly.

"It's gotten warmer out here than I'd expected," he said, modestly tugging his T-shirt over his bare chest again.

Hannah was sorry to see him do it. He had a very nice chest—again, not bulked up, but definitely well-toned and very lightly tanned. Though she really had no business noticing, she couldn't stop herself. Acting on her attraction was out of the question, but looking couldn't hurt, right?

"That's because you're working in full sunlight," she advised, more primly than she'd intended. "It's still nice and cool in the shade. But vegetables need more sun than shade to thrive, thus the location of the beds."

"I'm not complaining," he hastened to assure her. "It actually feels good to be out here with the sun on my face. Although I have to admit I've enjoyed the walks to the compost bin since it's in a shady spot."

"Only for another hour or so until the sun shifts, but the drive will be shaded by then so the walk itself won't be bad."

"In that case, the T-shirt is definitely coming off," he said with a grin.

"Come up to the house and have lunch first," Hannah offered. "And you really should put on some sunscreen, too. I keep a tube handy in the kitchen for me and Will."

"Good idea."

Evan set the hoe in the wheelbarrow and pulled off his gloves, then joined Hannah on the gravel drive.

"I thought I'd make sandwiches for lunch. I have ham and Swiss cheese and turkey, lettuce and tomato and whole wheat bread. And, of course, the old standby, peanut butter and jelly."

She glanced at him questioningly, hoping he wasn't a picky eater. Although he could always munch on one of the bagels he'd brought with him.

"I'm easy where food is concerned," he said. "I'm also especially fond of ham and cheese sandwiches."

"That's a relief."

As they climbed the porch steps, Will and Nellie jumped off the old-fashioned wooden swing, setting it rocking against the porch rail.

"Can we make the sandwiches now?" he asked eagerly.

"Yes, we can. But first be sure to wash your hands. And let's leave Nellie on the porch, okay? 'Cause her paws are kind of muddy."

"Okay, Mommy."

"I should probably take off my boots and leave them out here, too," Evan said.

"Good idea, but put them just inside the door so Nellie won't chew on them."

In the house, Hannah headed for the kitchen while Will and Evan peeled off in opposite directions to wash up. By the time they joined her again, she had the sandwich fixings laid upon the counter and was ready to start assembling meat, cheese, veggies, bread and condiments as requested.

"Ham and cheese for you, Evan. Right?"

"Yes, please," he replied, adding, "I can pour the drinks if you'd like."

"That would be a big help. Glasses in that cabinet," she advised with a nod of her head. "There's ice in the freezer, too. I'll have tea and I'd like Will to have a small glass of milk."

"Done."

"Do you want lettuce and tomato, mustard and mayo on your sandwich, too?"

"Lettuce, tomato and mustard," he said.

"How about you, Will? Ham or turkey or PB and J today?"

"Turkey…just plain turkey."

"Okay, just plain turkey for you."

Hannah put the sandwiches on plates, including a turkey with lettuce and tomato for herself, two each for her and Evan and one for Will. She carried them to the table along with a bag of chips she took from the pantry as Evan set their drinks on the table, as well.

So hungry were all three of them that they ate for several minutes in relative silence. Finally somewhat sated, Hannah looked up to see Evan eyeing her from across the table. He had spiked his short, blond hair with damp hands while upstairs, making him appear a little younger, a little…softer. A slight, quizzical smile also edged up the corners of his mouth.

"What?" she asked, afraid that she might have a bit of bread or a dot of mustard smeared on her face.

"I was just thinking how glad I am that I'm not the only one who's ravenous," he replied.

"What's…*rabanis?*" Will demanded, stuttering over the unfamiliar word.

"Very, very hungry," Hannah explained.

"Well, I'm *rabanis,* too."

Her son took another big bite of his sandwich.

"Not surprising for any of us. We all worked hard this morning—especially you, Evan. You've done an amazing job on the vegetable gardens in a really short time," Hannah said.

Evan's full mouth took on a more sheepish slant as he reached for his glass of iced tea, winced, then subtly rolled his shoulders.

"I hope you won't be too disappointed if I slow down some this afternoon. I'm starting to feel joints and muscles aching that I'd forgotten I even had."

"I'd be surprised if you didn't slow down a lot," Hannah assured him. "And it's perfectly all right. I'd much rather have you pace yourself than burn out in only a day."

"I don't think I'll burn out, but I can see that pacing is going to be a good idea."

"Maybe you should take a nap like me and Nellie," Will interjected. "Only I don't always fall asleep. Sometimes I talk to Nellie. But Nellie's paws are all muddy today so she might have to take *her* nap on the porch."

"I try not to take naps 'cause if I do, I have trouble sleeping at night. Although I have a feeling I'll be out like a light once my head hits the pillow tonight," Evan admitted in a wry tone.

"My daddy took a lot of naps," Will said. "We had to be real quiet so we wouldn't wake him up 'cause that made him mad. I don't get mad when I wake up from my nap, though. I get happy 'cause Mommy gives me cookies and milk for an afternoon snack."

Evan glanced at Hannah, a questioning look in his eyes again. She met his intense gaze for a moment, wondering what he must be thinking of her son's bald statement. She didn't want to explain to him about Stewart's behavior in front of Will—didn't want to drag that sad, frightening time into the peacefulness of the present moment.

But she should say something to smooth over the awkwardness between them, shouldn't she?

As if sensing her discomfort, Evan came to the rescue. Reaching out, he tweaked Will on the chin, making him giggle, then said, "Hey, for some of your mom's cookies, I'd take a nap any day, buddy."

"You are more than welcome to cookies and milk in the afternoon even without a nap first," Hannah said, grateful to him for so considerately putting her at ease again.

"That's one offer I plan to hold you to, regardless," Evan replied, a purely mischievous twinkle in his bright blue eyes.

"I promise not to renege." Slightly uncomfortable with the flutter his statement caused, Hannah waved a hand at his empty plate. "Would you like another sandwich or more chips?"

Sitting back in his chair, Evan patted his flat stomach with a hand and shook his head.

"I'm full, as I should be after eating both of those sandwiches you made. They were really good."

"And you were *rabanis,*" Will added.

"Yes, I most certainly was," Evan agreed.

Standing along with Hannah, he picked up his plate and glass and carried them to the sink, his hip bumping gently against hers as they paused there together.

"Oh, sorry," she said, suddenly embarrassed by their close proximity.

"I'm the one who should apologize for getting in your way. But I didn't want you to think I expected you to either wait on me or clean up after me."

"It's not like my kitchen's all that small. It's just that I'm so used to cooking and cleaning up around here on my own that having you help out threw me off just a little. I *could* get used to it, though," she acknowledged before she had time to really consider what she was saying.

"That's good to know because I'm here to help you any way I can," Evan said, again getting them past an awkward moment in a lighthearted manner. "Which means I'd better head back to the vegetable gardens and go to work again."

"Let me get the sunscreen for you." Hannah put a hand on his arm to stop him as he turned away. "You should probably wear a hat, too."

"Good idea," Evan replied. "I have a baseball cap in the Jeep. I'll be sure to grab it on my way down the drive."

Hannah took the tube of sunscreen off the shelf by the kitchen door that opened onto the wood deck. She had intended to give it to Evan and let him take it with him. But she hesitated a moment, remembering what he'd said about taking off his T-shirt when he went back to work. It was even warmer outdoors now, and without his shirt on, he'd be even more exposed to the more intense rays of the afternoon sun....

"I...I could rub some lotion on your back if you'd like," she offered in a tentative tone, afraid of appearing to be too forward. "That is, if you're going to take off your shirt later."

Evan met her gaze steadily, not saying anything for several long seconds, surprise and something else Hannah couldn't quite define evident in his eyes. Sure that she'd blundered badly, she felt her face flush. Embarrassed, she looked away and silently moved to set the tube of sunscreen on the table, wishing *she* could now be the one to think of a clever comment to ease the discomfort she'd caused between them this time. She was a thirty-two-year-old mother—a widow for heaven's sake—and yet here she was feeling as awkward as if it was her first date. Had the past few years changed her that much?

She already knew the answer.

"Hey, that's an offer I can't refuse," Evan said, his deep voice cutting into her thoughts as he caught her by the hand.

Glancing up at him, Hannah saw gentleness and encouragement in his eyes, as well, and felt her chagrin slowly fade away.

"I prefer working without a shirt when it's hot outdoors, but I don't want to risk a bad sunburn, especially on my back," he added, letting go of her hand to pull off his T-shirt.

"The sun can be pretty fierce up here even when the air is still cool," Hannah advised, fiddling with the cap

on the tube to keep from staring outright at his broad,
bare shoulders, smooth, muscular chest and flat ab-
domen.

Again she realized how strong and fit he was despite
his spare build. She wondered if he'd worked out with
weights in his other life, but didn't have the courage
to ask. In fact, finding the courage to squeeze a dollop
of sunscreen out of the tube and onto her fingertips as
he turned away from her, then reach out and begin
rubbing it onto his equally smooth and muscular back
was about as much as she could handle at the moment.

At the first touch of her fingers to his bare skin,
Evan flinched, causing Hannah to make a startled
movement, as well.

"Sorry—" she began, pulling her hand away. "Did
I do something to—"

"Not at all," he assured her, glancing over his shoulder at her and offering her a wry smile. "The lotion just
felt a little cool against my skin."

"Oh, I didn't think about that," she murmured
apologetically.

"It didn't feel bad. It just took me by surprise," Evan
said, glancing at her again, his smile widening. "A little friction between your fingers and my bare skin and
I believe that lotion will warm up very nicely."

It wasn't only the lotion that warmed up nicely as
Hannah rubbed it carefully into Evan's bare back. Her
face grew hotter by the moment as unexpected and
quite unseemly thoughts of fingers, friction and bare
skin danced unbidden into her head.

Years had passed since she and Stewart had last
shared a close, physically intimate relationship. She
had learned over time to direct her sexual energy into

other things until it dissipated—caring for Stewart, for Will, the house, the gardens when she could. For longer than she could remember, she had been sure that she would never experience sexual desire again.

But obviously the wanting, the needing to be held by a man, to be kissed and caressed with an equally strong want and need hadn't really disappeared as she'd supposed. Apparently her want and need had simply been sublimated, lurking in her subconscious, ready and waiting for just the right stimulation to come along.

"Mommy, you have a funny look on your face," Will announced, startling Hannah out of her reverie with the thoroughness of a splash of icy water. "Are you sleepy?"

Aware that she had likely been rubbing Evan Graham's back far longer than absolutely necessary, Hannah pulled her hand away, blushed even more deeply and gazed at her son with dismay.

"Sleepy?"

"Yes, Mommy. Your eyes were kind of closing."

"Oh, well, I was just…thinking about…some things," she said, knowing that Evan was now looking at her curiously, too.

She couldn't believe she had succumbed so completely to the unexpected allure of his masculinity. He'd only taken off his shirt, for goodness sake, and she'd only been applying a film of sunscreen to his back.

Evan was a nice guy—his kindness in smoothing over their awkward moments had proven that. But nice didn't equal interested. She couldn't afford to mistake the two.

Hannah risked a glance at him, and wondered, first, if he had any idea of the trail her thoughts had been taking, then hoped against hope that he hadn't. He met her gaze, his expression reassuringly bland until Will piped up again.

"Must have been pretty good things, Mommy, 'cause you looked happy, too."

"Um, yes," she admitted, focusing her attention on replacing the cap on the tube of sunscreen, but not before she glimpsed the knowing smile suddenly sketched across Evan's handsome face.

There was no doubt in Hannah's mind then that the man had been conscious to some degree of how her demeanor had altered. The brisk, businesslike rub of a hand was entirely different from a slow caress—as well as easily discernible by the recipient. And no matter how she wished she could deny it, she had definitely been caressing Evan Graham's back only a few moments ago.

"Time for me to get back to work," he said, pulling his T-shirt on again.

"Me, too, after I get Will settled in for his nap," Hannah agreed. "Take the sunscreen with you and don't forget your cap."

"Yes, ma'am."

Evan winked at her as he took the tube of sunscreen she held out to him, then turned to head out the side door.

"Do I *have* to take a nap today, Mommy?" Will asked as he did most every day, jumping out of his chair.

"Just a short one, okay? Otherwise you'll be really tired later…cranky, too, and that's no fun at all," Hannah reminded him, trying to get Evan's wink out of her mind.

"Okay, but just *one* hour."

"One hour, it is," she agreed. "Go wash your hands, then take off your shoes and climb into bed."

"Can Nellie have a nap with me? Please, Mommy, *please.*"

"Let me see how much it's going to be to get her cleaned off." Luckily, the dog had stayed on the porch while they ate lunch. Luckily, too, the mud on her paws had dried enough so that it flaked off easily enough. Thus one less battle before Will settled down to rest was eliminated.

With boy and dog stretched out on Will's twin bed, Hannah returned to the kitchen to wash the dishes they'd used at lunch. The task usually required only a few minutes of her time. But that afternoon she lingered far longer than necessary, fingers sifting through the froth of soap bubbles atop the sink full of warm water, her thoughts miles away.

Well, not *miles* away, she acknowledged when at last she pulled the stopper and let the now brackish water drain away. More like a few hundred yards or so—just down the drive to the vegetable gardens where Evan Graham was working, likely with his shirt off, his bare chest bronzing in the sun....

Giving herself a firm mental shake, Hannah left the dishes to dry on the drain board and stepped out the back door onto the deck. She had better things to do than moon over Evan Graham.

Okay, maybe not necessarily *better,* but certainly more productive. And just then being productive was the *best* thing she could think of to do.

Chapter Four

"That was an excellent meal, Hannah," Evan said, trying not to wince too noticeably as he stood, picked up his plate, silverware and glass and started across the kitchen to the sink. "Eggplant Parmesan is a favorite of mine and I haven't had any as good as yours, even in a fancy, high-priced restaurant. Your Italian salad was wonderful, too."

"Thanks a lot," Hannah replied. She paused to collect Will's dishes as well as her own before joining him at the sink. "I have another pan of it in the freezer so it will definitely be on the menu again. In a few weeks we'll have lettuce fresh from the garden for our salads, too. You'll be amazed at how much better it is than store-bought."

"Worth all the hard work, huh?" he asked.

Turning on the faucet, he rinsed the plates, then taking the initiative even further, he plugged the sink and poured in a dollop of dish detergent.

"Just wait and see," she said, adding as he put the dishes in the hot, soapy water, "Hey, you don't have to do the dishes for me."

Wincing inwardly, this time as a result of the pang of guilt Hannah's sprightly "just wait and see" had caused him, Evan scrubbed a plate with the dishcloth.

"You cooked. Let me at least help a little with the cleanup," he requested with a smile.

"I mostly chopped lettuce, sliced onions and tomatoes, and slid the casserole dish in the oven. You worked hard all day, clearing beds and hauling debris to the compost bin."

"You worked hard, too, moving all those seedlings out of the greenhouses and onto the deck."

"I worked hard, too, didn't I, Mommy?" Will demanded, bouncing over to the sink, empty glass in hand. "And I finished all my milk. Can I please watch television now?"

"Yes, you worked hard, too, and thank you for finishing all your milk, and yes, you *may* watch television, but only for one hour."

"Thank you, Mommy."

Mother and son exchanged a quick hug, then Will bounded off to the living room, the ever-faithful Nellie close at his heels. Taking a clean towel from the drawer and selecting a dish from the drain board to dry, Hannah seemed to accept his offer without further argument.

"He's a really good child, isn't he?" Evan asked, voicing his thought aloud after they had worked together for a few minutes in silence. "Very bright and well-adjusted."

"Do I detect the faintest hint of surprise in your voice?" Hannah quizzed in return, only half-teasingly.

Glancing at her, Evan saw that beneath her pleasant demeanor, her steady gaze held a very definite challenge in it. He could lie to her, as he already was in so many ways that could prove to be hurtful, or make an attempt at being honest. Since he only lied out of absolute necessity in order to get a job done, he chose now to tell the truth.

"Yes, actually, I'm *sure* you did," he said, focusing his attention on the sink full of dirty dishes submerged in the soapy water. "You're a widow on you own here, raising your son without any help. Both you and Will have had to deal with the death of your husband, his father. That has to have taken an emotional toll on the two of you. Grief can often lead to anger and depression that can then be directed at an innocent party. I've seen that happen in the past, but I don't see any indication of that happening with you and Will."

Several beats of silence followed Evan's comments causing him to glance again at Hannah. She wasn't looking at him, but staring instead at the plate she held, continuing to rub it with her towel though it had already been thoroughly dried. The corners of her mouth turned down in a thoughtful frown, as she seemed to search for a reasonable reply.

"My husband was…ill for a long time," she said at last, glancing up at him, then quickly away again. "By the time he died…we'd had time to accept that we were losing him." She hesitated, took a deep breath, then continued quietly. "We *did* grieve for him. But his death was also a blessing for…all of us. I think that made it a little easier for us to cope with our sadness. It helped, too, that Will was old enough at the time to understand a lot of…things." She paused again, finally set aside the plate and reached for another. "As you said, he's very bright and well-adjusted. I'm very lucky in that respect."

"He's lucky, too, Hannah—you're a very bright, very loving and understanding mother." And a fascinating woman, Evan silently noted.

"I appreciate the compliment, but are you sure you've known me long enough to make that kind of assumption," she asked with another glance at him, half-teasing once again.

"Actually, I've had more experience with other sorts of mothers—the ones who are incapable of making a kind, understanding, loving gesture toward their children, either out of ignorance or unwillingness," Evan answered, opting for honesty a second time.

Understandably, Hannah's eyes widened with surprise. Evan could almost see the mental gears turning in her pretty head. He could also easily imagine all the questions forming in her mind, and cursed himself for being careless. Too much truthfulness often opened doors better left closed—and stirred up matters best left alone. Matters involving his identity and the real reason he had accepted minimum wage and room-and-board to work for her as a gardener.

He didn't want to lie to Hannah to cover for his blunder. Nor did he have the energy to glibly dance around the truth. So he continued quickly in a matter-of-fact tone as he rinsed the last of the silverware and put it in the plastic basket on the drain board.

"That's why it's really heartening to meet someone who hasn't let loss get the better of her."

"I didn't really consider that I had a choice," she said. "I had to think about Will and put his needs ahead of mine. That's what mothers do, isn't it?"

"Good mothers."

Evan pulled the stopper from the sink and ran water from the faucet to rinse away the last of the soap bubbles. He kept his eyes averted, as well, hoping to discourage any further discussion on the topic.

"Well, I try my best—"

"And you seem to be succeeding," he acknowledged, then immediately changed the subject, asking, "Need any help with anything else before I go upstairs?"

"You've helped more than enough already for one day," Hannah replied, her gratitude more than evident in her voice.

"I'd better call it a night, then, or I doubt I'll be good for anything in the morning."

Hannah's smile turned sympathetic as she folded her towel and hung it on the rack above the sink.

"You looked like you were feeling a bit stiff and sore when you got up from the table a few minutes ago."

"And here I thought I'd hidden it so well," he said dryly.

"I would have guessed it even if you hadn't had that pained expression on your face. Weeding a vegetable garden uses muscles that don't get much of a workout sitting in front of a computer screen eight hours a day."

"You can say that again."

"Do you have something you can take to ease the aches?"

"I have some ibuprofen tablets. I imagine a dose or two will help a lot, along with some icy-hot gel."

For just an instant, Evan thought—actually *hoped*—Hannah would offer to help with the icy-hot gel he'd wisely brought with him as she had with the sunscreen earlier. He had liked the way she'd touched him, then—the stroke of her hand on his bare skin gentle and caressing. In fact, he'd liked it more than he had a right to under the circumstances. But then, it had been a very long time since he'd experienced the tenderness of a woman's touch. And though he admitted to himself that it wouldn't be a good idea to encourage a repeat performance, he wouldn't have refused an offer if she'd made one.

But Hannah swiftly shifted her gaze, shoving her hands safely in the side pockets of her jeans as her face flushed bright red.

"Well, you'll probably want to use it, too."

"Oh, I agree."

"I guess I'll see you in the morning, then. I'll have breakfast ready about seven-thirty, but you're welcome to come downstairs earlier and put on a pot of coffee. You're also welcome to rustle up a bowl of cereal or eat a bagel if you'd like."

"Seven-thirty sounds fine to me. I should be able to drag my aching bones out of bed by then."

Evan turned away and started across the kitchen. Then he remembered the one question he'd meant to ask her earlier. Pausing, he turned back to her again.

"I was wondering if it would be all right to plug into the phone jack upstairs with my computer modem so I can go online," he said. "I've already checked with my server and there's a local number available for this area. So I wouldn't be running up any long distance charges on your telephone bill."

Evan had found that using his cell phone was almost impossible so far out in the country and mountains. And he didn't want to risk having Hannah or Will overhear him in conversation with his assistant at the office by using her landline, either. That left e-mail as his best bet for keeping in touch with his office in the days ahead.

"That's fine with me," Hannah assured him.

"I promise not to tie up your telephone line for too long at a time. And if I'm online and you want to make a call or log onto the Internet yourself, just let me know."

"I don't make many calls and I rarely go online, so I don't foresee there being any problem. I mostly look at Web sites for other growers in the area to get an idea of what they're charging for their plants, but I haven't had a lot of time to do that lately."

"Have you ever thought of setting up a Web site of your own?" Evan asked.

"Yes, but I wasn't sure until now that I'd have anything to sell on it this year," she said. "Plus, I haven't the first clue how to put together a Web site, and I wasn't sure that it would be worth the expense of having someone else do it for me."

"I could do it for you," Evan said before he had a chance to really consider the ramifications of digging himself deeper into Hannah James's life.

Once the words had left his mouth, he was sure he'd eventually come to regret saying them aloud. But the surprise and delight in Hannah's eyes made it impossible for him to equivocate in any way on his initial offer.

"That would be wonderful," she said, her pleasure echoing in her smile for an instant, then fading as a frown creased her forehead. "But I want to pay you, and I'm not sure—"

"You can pay me the same hourly wage you're paying for the gardening work," Evan hastened to say, attempting to alleviate somewhat the additional twinges of conscience he was suddenly experiencing.

A quick calculation of the time it would take him to set up Hannah's Web site at minimum wage per hour assured him that the work involved would be more of a gift to her than anything else.

"I'm sure you could get much more money for that kind of technical work," she demurred, still looking rather pensive.

"Hannah," he said gently, "it's really not a problem. I wouldn't have offered it if it wasn't okay." Seeing her expression brighten, he added, "I'll do a little research in the evening over the next week or so, and then I can get to work on it when you have an idea of what plants you want to sell and when they'll be available."

"Just be sure to keep track of your time, okay?"

"I will."

"Please don't feel like you have to start on it right away, either. I know you're exhausted and you likely will be until you're more used to working in the gardens," Hannah said. "In fact, working on the Web site would be a great rainy day project. We'll be having lots of those the next few weeks."

"April showers?"

"May showers, too, and June, July and August," she advised with a wry smile. "That's why we have such good luck with everything we grow here."

"Well, then, the Web site can be a rainy day project for sure." Evan smiled, too, then finally turned away again. "I'd better head upstairs now so you and Will can spend some time together."

He didn't add that he wanted to get the climb up the narrow staircase over with before the muscles in his thighs tightened up completely.

"His television time is just about up and he definitely needs a bath before bed tonight," Hannah said, following him into the living room.

"Good night, Will." Evan ruffled a hand over the boy's thick, dark hair, distracting him from the family-oriented sitcom he was watching for only a nanosecond.

"Good night, Mr. Graham."

"Good night to you, too, Hannah," Evan added, pausing for a last moment at the foot of the staircase to glance back at her as she chased Nellie off the sofa, then sat down there herself.

"Have a good sleep," she replied.

"Oh, I'm sure I will. See you in the morning."

Evan made it up the stairs without actually groaning aloud, but it wasn't easy. Regular workouts at the gym and twice- or thrice-weekly runs in the park apparently hadn't provided him with quite as much physical conditioning as he'd thought. He seemed to have become stiff and sore in even more unexpected places as the evening had progressed. The only help for it was a hot shower, a dose of ibuprofen and the best rubdown he could manage to give himself with the pain-relief gel he'd bought at a pharmacy in Boone last night.

In his room, Evan unpacked only the absolute necessities—toiletries, a clean T-shirt, boxers and sweatpants to sleep in, and socks and a shirt to put on in the morning. Although slightly muddy around the lower legs, the jeans he'd worn that day would have to do for at least another day or two, until he could buy more appropriate work clothes. At the time he'd packed his bag, he hadn't really expected to stay in the area more than a few days—a week at the most. And he certainly hadn't expected to actually go to work for Hannah James, preparing garden areas to be planted.

Of course, he wouldn't have to worry about having enough clean clothes if he left at the end of the week as he'd planned to yesterday, Evan reminded himself as he turned on the faucet in the shower stall.

With a twist of his lips, he stripped off his clothes as the water heated up, then stepped under the steamy spray with a sigh of intensely grateful pleasure. Even without the added job of setting up a Web site, he couldn't see himself walking out on Hannah and Will—not with so much work yet to be completed in the gardens.

There was no telling how long it might take her to find someone else willing to work for what she could afford to pay or what kind of person he might be. Evan didn't like the thought of some slick, smooth-tongued devil with an ulterior motive up his sleeve taking residence in her house.

Granted, she already had one of *those* living with her, he admitted as he finally shut off the water, grabbed a towel and rubbed at his chest and upper arms with it.

He was going to help her as much as he could, he decided firmly. He'd stay a few weeks longer than he'd originally planned, help her get her gardens cleared and planted and set up her Web site. Otherwise there would be no assuaging his guilty conscience.

Plus, he could make sure Will was okay.

He could keep in touch with the office and the investigators who worked for him via e-mail. If need be, he could also make some excuse to Hannah and drive down to Charlotte for a day to personally handle anything out of the ordinary. As for his staff, he'd just say he was on vacation—he was certainly entitled to one.

Not that anyone on his staff would give him any grief about it. He was the boss, after all, and they would probably welcome a respite from his hard-to-break bad habit of micromanaging every case he accepted.

With a dose of ibuprofen taken and his muscles beginning to loosen just a bit from the icy-hot gel, Evan pulled on his T-shirt and sweatpants, then eyed the laptop he'd left on the desk. He needed to e-mail his assistant, Melanie—or Mel as she preferred to be called—and let her know about the problem with the cell phone reception here in the mountains. If she had been trying to reach him by phone today, she would be concerned, especially if she didn't have an explanatory e-mail from him in the morning.

Exhausted, the last thing Evan wanted to do just then was go online and write an e-mail. He had no choice, though—not only did they need to know where he was, but how to run interference for him with Randall James should the need arise.

Having now spent an entire day with Hannah and Will, Evan believed even more firmly that he had been hired by her former father-in-law under false pretenses. She had yet to exhibit any signs at all that she was an unfit mother in need of psychiatric care, and from the well-adjusted attitude she and her son exhibited, he doubted that she ever would.

Although there *had* been an odd hitch in her voice whenever she'd spoken of her husband, Evan acknowledged thoughtfully as he eased into the desk chair and turned on his computer.

Hannah had seemed to choose her words carefully in regard to Stewart James. Possibly due to Will's close proximity during their conversation as to any other reason, nefarious or not.

He wasn't there to analyze Hannah James's relationship with her dead husband, though. His job was to assess her competency as a mother. So far, he hadn't seen or heard anything to confirm Randall James's accusations to the contrary.

Still, Evan wanted to know *why* Randall's feelings for Hannah were so negative. Was he merely one of those old-school stuffed shirts who were scornful of anyone they considered beneath them in social status? Or was he the one who was dangerously psychotic?

Snobbery wasn't a concern—he was more than able to put Randall James in his place. But if Randall intended to pose any kind of threat to Hannah or to Will, regardless of Evan's view of the situation, then the man would dismiss him from the investigation in a minute, then possibly hire someone else less scrupulous to do his dirty work.

Acknowledging that he had yet another reason to stay close to Hannah awhile longer, Evan scanned his incoming e-mail and found nothing that required his immediate attention. He typed a message to Mel detailing his plans for the next few days, then shut off the computer with a weary sigh. A glance at the clock on the desk told him it wasn't quite nine o'clock, but he was suddenly so tired he wanted only to crawl under the quilt on the bed and sleep for at least a week.

Only when Evan had turned out the light on the nightstand did he realize just how dark a night in the country could be. He couldn't recall a time when he'd been so far away from the lights and the noise of a city. Nor could he remember a time when he'd felt so…disconnected from the normal hustle and bustle of the life he led.

But lying there in the upstairs bedroom of Hannah's house, staring into the darkness, the surprising truth of it was he didn't miss his big-city life at all just then. While he had a perfectly satisfying job and existence back in Charlotte, somehow being here at Hannah's offered the possibility for *connection.* One that he hadn't realized—until now—was missing in his life.

He had told Hannah that he'd come to the mountains of North Carolina looking for a change of pace as well as a change of place. He'd meant it only as a cover story to enable his investigation. But maybe there had been more truth to his casual comment than he'd realized.

Of course, there was always a possibility that he was simply too tired to think straight at the moment. Evan had always been a loner by nature. He also knew better than to get personally involved with anyone related to a case he was handling. He had never done that in the past, and he couldn't in good conscience do it now. Not that he *wanted* to get personally involved with Hannah James. He just wanted to give her a hand with her gardens and her Web site. And then—when he was sure she and her son would be okay—he'd make up some excuse and go back where he belonged.

Chapter Five

Standing at the stove early Friday morning, ladling pancake batter onto the hot griddle, Hannah caught herself humming along with the theme song of her son's favorite weekday program coming from the living room where Will sat in front of the television. Outside the kitchen windows, rays of sunlight had begun to filter through the trees, offering the promise of another warm, clear day. It was the fourth in a row since Tuesday when Evan Graham had started working for her.

She couldn't believe how much they had accomplished together in that short period of time, especially considering the fact that Evan was a novice gardener and had also been really stiff and sore on Wednesday. He hadn't complained at all, but one look at the stoic face he presented at breakfast that morning, and Hannah had known that he was suffering from myriad aches and pains, all the result of his concentrated effort to clear the vegetable beds on Tuesday.

Afraid that he might have a change of heart about the job he'd taken, despite his expressed need for a place to stay, she had urged him to take it easy on Wednesday. But Evan had insisted that he would be better off working out the kinks in his joints and muscles than risking the possibility that his body would stiffen up even more from inactivity. And though she had offered him the less strenuous task of starting another batch of seedlings in the greenhouse, he had chosen instead to work on clearing the remainder of the beds.

"You said that's the top priority right now," he had reminded her.

"Yes, it is," she'd agreed. "More important than starting more seedlings. We can do that on the next rainy day we have." Hannah had paused a moment, thinking quickly of how best to keep him from pushing himself too hard. Then she had added brightly, "In fact, with the weather so nice we might as well *all* focus on the vegetable gardens today."

Evan had shot her a wry look, obviously aware of her play. But he hadn't argued with her, and he had seemed more than happy to go along with the slow, steady pace she'd set both Wednesday and Thursday.

As a result, the beds for the vegetables were now completely cleared and ready for them to start turning compost into the soil—another physically demanding job. But doing it together, even at the same slow and steady pace they'd developed over the past couple of days, they should be done with it by that evening.

Smiling slightly as she layered the first stack of pancakes on a platter, then slid it into the oven beside the platter of crisp cooked bacon already there to keep warm, Hannah thought about how much she had enjoyed working side by side with Evan. He was such good company—such a contrast to the last man she'd lived with. Not that they talked about much more than her plans for the gardens.

He seemed genuinely interested in where she intended to plant the various vegetables she wanted to grow, as well as why. And she had been more than happy to share with him her knowledge and experience.

She had only answered the questions he'd voiced aloud, though.

When Evan had also seemed interested in when she might be able to start selling produce as well as plants, Hannah initially had assumed that he'd needed that information to factor into his plans for her Web site. But then she had sensed that perhaps he also had another, underlying concern, perhaps about her financial situation.

She hoped that he wasn't worried about her. She wasn't in danger of becoming destitute. Yet at the same time her heart warmed at the thought that Evan might care about her enough to be concerned on her behalf.

The creak of the staircase as Evan descended not only coincided with the completion of Hannah's last batch of pancakes, but also effectively ended her reverie. Not that she minded. She would rather enjoy having Evan Graham with her in the kitchen than merely *think* about him any day.

That realization, quickly followed by an unexpected, vivid image of Evan pressing her back against the counter and taking control of her mouth with his, made her stomach flutter with a mix of sexual awareness, anticipation and uncertainty. Was it a good idea to have become so…*attached* to someone she had only known for a few days, someone who might not be as honest or as forthright as she hoped? Who could up and leave any time he chose for no good reason at all?

Someone who made her feel things she thought were dead.

Although *attached* might be too strong a word to describe how she felt about Evan Graham, Hannah demurred. *Attached* implied a bond of a deeper, more durable and dependable kind that only really came with emotional, and eventually, physical intimacy. Her relationship with Evan hadn't reached either stage yet, and considering how self-contained he seemed to be— and that an affair was the absolute last thing she needed—it likely wouldn't any time soon.

While he had seemed relatively open about himself during his initial interview, Hannah couldn't say that she'd learned anything new about him, personally, in the past four days.

"Hey, buddy, what's that big yellow bird up to today?" Evan cheerfully asked Will.

"A, B, C's and one, two, threes—the same as yesterday," she heard Will reply with a giggle.

"No X, Y, Z's and eight, nine, tens?" Evan teased.

"Some of those, too."

Hannah took the warm platters full of pancakes and bacon from the oven, set them on the kitchen table and joined Evan and her son in the living room. Evan shifted his gaze from the television screen to her and acknowledged her with a slight smile.

"Something smells really good," he said.

"Pancakes and bacon," she advised him, allowing herself to enjoy a moment of feminine pleasure at the masculine appreciation she saw in his eyes. She also noted, yet again, how attractive he was first thing in the morning, freshly showered and shaved and looking rested and relaxed. Then, feeling suddenly shy, she turned her attention to Will, adding, "Time to turn off the television, kiddo, and come eat your breakfast."

"Okay, Mommy," he replied reluctantly, switching off the TV.

As Hannah returned to the kitchen and poured juice and milk, Evan refilled her coffee mug, then helped himself to a mug, as well. The past couple of mornings they had bantered back and forth a bit about mundane things like the weather or Nellie's whereabouts—out on the porch that particular morning—or the heartiness of their appetites. But today Evan seemed a little quieter than usual, and the glance he aimed in her direction as he sat across the table from her seemed to hold a slight yet still noticeable measure of apprehension.

As they helped themselves to pancakes and bacon from the platters on the table, Hannah's overactive imagination immediately shifted into overdrive, presenting her with half a dozen worst-case scenarios. Unfortunately, each of her scenarios featured a different version of Evan telling her something that she didn't want to hear—something that would force her to have to let him go or some excuse he would make to leave on his own.

She'd been foolishly fantasizing about a heated

kitchen encounter with a man she barely knew when she should have been focusing on her fledgling business—and her only hope of building any kind of life for her and Will. Hadn't the past taught her anything about useless romantic notions?

She had never had a tendency toward paranoia, Hannah reminded herself as she poured warm syrup on her short stack of pancakes, then passed the pitcher to Evan. And neither did she have any good, solid reason to panic at the prospect of losing him. Financially she needed him, but she and Will would find a way to get by if they had to, she decided. And considering the newness of their relationship, *losing,* like *attached,* seemed an inappropriate concept for her to be entertaining with such…exaggerated emotion. Evan was *just* an employee. Albeit a handsome employee…but nothing more.

"You've outdone yourself again this morning, Hannah," Evan said, gesturing with his fork to the already half-eaten stack of pancakes and the remaining slice of the four slices of bacon that he'd originally served himself remaining on his plate.

"I thought we all deserved something more substantial than cereal since we'll be composting the vegetable beds today. We have a lot of shoveling and hauling and shoveling again ahead of us. But we should be able to finish it before dark. Then I propose we all take the weekend off."

"Can we go to town on Saturday, Mommy? Can we, *please?*" Will asked with undisguised excitement. "I want to get some storybooks at the library and eat pizza for lunch at Mellow Mushroom."

"Yes, we can go to town tomorrow," Hannah agreed.

"Can Mr. Graham come with us, too?"

"He's welcome to come with us," she answered her son. Then looking at Evan, she added, "More than welcome…."

"I'd really like to join you, but…"

He met Hannah's gaze for a long moment, then looked down at his plate as he twirled a last slice of pancake in a last dollop of syrup with his fork.

"We'll understand if you'd rather hang out here and relax, or take off somewhere on your own," Hannah hastened to assure him as the panicky feeling she'd been feeling ratcheted up another notch.

She had been expecting him to say something she wouldn't like since they'd sat down at the table, and now he finally was. She wasn't really surprised—what you thought was more often than not what you got. But she was more than a little disappointed—in Evan as well as in herself. She had hoped he wouldn't let her down, but his doing so wasn't what she could rightly define as a devastating experience. And she knew devastating experiences firsthand.

"Actually, I've had…something come up. Some… personal business that I need to take care of in…Charlotte later this afternoon," Evan advised with another surreptitious glance her way. "I'll have to leave here at noon, and I many not be back until tomorrow." He paused, looked at her again and this time held her gaze. "I'm really sorry to have to let you down today. I know you wanted to finish the composting and you won't be able to do it on your own. I don't want you to even *try,* either. I can, and will, finish up on Saturday no matter what time I get back here."

Hannah realized almost at once that while it had

been nerve-racking to imagine Evan walking out on her, the reality carried with it an odd measure of relief. She had always hated having the feeling that she was waiting for the other shoe to drop. In fact, to her way of thinking, there were few things worse than the growing anticipation of something awful about to happen.

And Evan *had* said that he would be back no later than tomorrow, she reminded herself as she pasted an understanding smile on her face. If, indeed, he chose to honor that intention once he'd finished his business in the city. She wasn't especially pleased with how much she hoped he would. She shouldn't allow herself to need him so much—but she did.

"Not to worry," she assured him, making an effort to balance sympathy with good humor as she pushed away from the table and began to gather their plates and silverware. "Business is…business. We all have to take care of it at one time or another, and unfortunately we can't always choose the when and the where." She placed the dishes in the sink and began to run the water.

"Believe me, Hannah, I wouldn't go to Charlotte today if I had a choice," Evan said so matter-of-factly that her doubts eased just a little.

"You don't have to wait until noon to leave," she told him with an unexpected surge of generosity as she began to wash the dishes. "And you certainly don't have to rush back here tomorrow. It's not like composting is a matter of life or death. I never meant for you to have to work on weekends, either."

"I appreciate your understanding—really, I do. But I can easily make my afternoon appointment if I leave here about twelve o'clock, and I don't mind making up the work I won't be able to do for you today on Saturday. Your summer income depends on how soon you have plants and produce ready to sell. Though not exactly a life or death issue, I know it's important to you in a lot of ways."

Evan was right, Hannah thought. Being able to earn some money during the summer was important to her. She didn't want to be an ogre about the prep work that still needed to be done, but she couldn't really afford to let Evan take the whole day off if he was willing to work at least half of it.

"Well, while I've turned compost into the soil on my own more times than I can count, I'm certainly not going to turn down the help."

"I helped you last summer, didn't I, Mommy?" Will piped up from his place at the table.

"You helped me a lot, sweetie." She smiled at her son, then added, "And I know you're going to help us a lot today, too. Just as soon as you finish your milk, okay?"

"Okay, Mommy."

"I guess I'd better head out to the shed and start filling the wheelbarrow with the first load of compost," Evan said as he stowed the plates he'd dried on a shelf in the cabinet, then hung his towel on the rack.

"Start with the mulch in the right-hand bin," Hannah instructed. "I'll meet you down by the vegetable beds in a few minutes and show you how to work it into the soil."

"See you there."

Hannah was gratified that Evan hadn't left for his appointment in Charlotte immediately as she'd suggested. Yet she still couldn't set aside completely a niggle of uncertainty about his eventual return once he'd taken care of his business—if, in fact, he *had* business in Charlotte.

"I'm ready, Mommy," Will said, holding out his empty glass to her.

"Good boy. Now get your jacket and put it on. It's a little chilly outside," Hannah told him as she dunked the glass in the last of the soapy water, rinsed it and set it on the drain board.

"I like it when it's chilly outside."

"Me, too, sweetie."

"Ready, Mommy?"

"All ready now."

Hannah wiped her hands on a towel and followed after Will to the side door. She took her own jacket from the peg and slipped into it, then the two of them stepped onto the porch where they were duly greeted by Nellie, wagging and wriggling as usual.

Not one to waste time, as Hannah had quickly discovered, Evan was already on his way down the driveway with the first wheelbarrow full of fresh compost, steaming in the cool morning air.

"Hey, that was fast," she called out, hurrying along with Will and the dog to catch up with him.

"I'd like to get as much of the composting done as I can before I leave for Charlotte." Evan paused by the first of the beds and glanced back at her. "Okay, now what?"

Hannah grabbed one of the shovels he had balanced atop the mound of dark, rich, earthy-smelling compost in the wheelbarrow.

"Now we shovel the compost onto the bed liberally and evenly, and work it into the top one or two inches of the soil," she replied, demonstrating as she talked with the ease of one who'd had years of hands-on experience.

"Can I help with the compost, too, Mommy?" Will asked eagerly.

"Yes, you *may.*"

"I brought your shovel," Evan said, handing the boy the smaller implement he'd included along with the larger ones for Hannah and him. Then he set to work, as well, following Hannah's lead.

By noon the three of them had managed to add compost to all but two of the beds Hannah would be using for her vegetables. They had shed their jackets shortly after starting the job and were soon rolling up their sleeves and wiping their sweaty foreheads. Still, they worked steadily, mostly in silence.

Occasionally, one or another of them would make a comment, and of course, Will took frequent breaks to scrutinize the long, pale red earthworms they came across as they turned the damp soil.

Evan's surprise at how many they saw had Hannah smiling as she patiently explained that seeing such a large number of the little critters was very fortunate, indeed.

"They are called nature's plow and they are definitely our gardening allies," she advised him. "We need to be careful not to harm them as we work the compost into the soil."

"What do they do that's so helpful?" Evan asked, his interest obvious.

"As they burrow through the soil, they loosen it, admitting air and water and helping the plants' roots to grow. Also, the organic matter that passes through their bodies is excreted in granular casings that are rich in nutrients the plants wouldn't get otherwise."

"You really know a lot about this gardening stuff, don't you?"

Pausing in the act of stowing his shovel in the empty wheelbarrow, Evan eyed Hannah with high regard. Pleased by his recognition—and unfamiliar with being on the receiving end of a man's respect—she blushed and looked away.

"I started out helping my mother in *her* gardens when I was about Will's age."

She, too, put her shovel in the wheelbarrow. Then she started up the driveway to the shed with Evan as he pushed the wheelbarrow, Will and Nellie racing along ahead of them.

"Obviously you must have enjoyed it," Evan said.

"Amazingly, I did, but my mother made it easy. She was very patient with me. She never gave me a job I couldn't handle and she never expected me to work long hours. She also made it a point to explain *everything* to me in terms I could understand. This land belonged to her family for generations. She valued it greatly. She also took good care of it, and taught me to do the same.

"But she also wanted me to expand my horizons. She saved the money she made from her plants and produce so that I could go to college and earn a degree in education. And she insisted that I live in Boone when I got my first job teaching elementary school. I didn't move back here until both of my parents became ill, almost seven years ago."

"I can understand even better now why you've decided to stay here," Evan acknowledged as they came up to the shed.

"There's nowhere else I'd rather be," Hannah admitted with a slight smile. "Hopefully, I'll never have to leave."

"I'd hate to see that happen," Evan said as he parked the wheelbarrow, then gazed at the thick forest that seemed to cocoon them in its stately beauty.

"Me, too." Hannah glanced up at the sky, measuring the slant of the sun, then added, "I'd also hate to see you miss your appointment in Charlotte, and it's already past noon."

Still looking off into the distance, Evan frowned. Then he gave a single, negative shake of his head, as if clearing away an unwanted thought.

"Yes, I'd better get on the road," he agreed, shifting his gaze to meet hers.

To Hannah's surprise, he also reached out and put his hands on her shoulders, his grip firm but gentle as he continued.

"But before I go, I want you to promise me that you won't attempt to finish composting the vegetable beds on your own."

"I can do it—" she began to protest.

"I know you can," he interrupted, giving her shoulders a little squeeze to emphasize his words. Shivers of excitement raced up her arms in response. "But it's one of the jobs you hired me to do, and I'll be back to do it by noon tomorrow at the latest. Take the afternoon off and do something fun with Will, okay?"

"Okay…" she agreed, mesmerized not only by the touch of his hands on her shoulders, but also by the piercing intensity of his bright blue eyes.

"Promise me?"

"I promise."

"Good deal." He gave her shoulders another gentle squeeze, and added, "Now I'd better hit the road."

"You…you *are* coming back, aren't you?" Hannah asked, putting her hand on his arm, unable to let him leave without extracting an assurance from him, as well.

"Yes, of course I'm coming back." He rested his hand atop hers for a moment before she let him go. "Hopefully tonight, but tomorrow at the very latest." Turning away he added, "I'll just run upstairs and get my key and be on my way."

"I hope you'll have a safe trip."

"I will."

Hannah watched Evan climb the porch steps, pause for a few moments to say something to Will, then go inside the house. Intent on keeping the promise she'd made, she stowed the wheelbarrow and shovels in the shed. By the time she reached the porch, Evan was on his way out again, his keys jangling in his hand, his face freshly scrubbed and his hair neatly combed.

"Do something fun for me this afternoon," he said, lightly brushing the back of his hand against her cheek for just an instant.

Though his gesture startled Hannah, Evan had made it so naturally that she didn't shy away. Instead she shot him a shy smile, her skin tingling from the warmth and tenderness of his touch.

"I will—I promise," she said. "Take care, Evan."

"You, too, Hannah."

She stood on the porch long after the sound of the Jeep's tires crunching on the gravel driveway had faded away. Only when Will tugged at her hand impatiently did she finally turn to go inside the house.

"Can I help you make lunch, Mommy?"

"I appreciate the offer, but I was thinking we could go into town for lunch today and then maybe see a movie." She'd planned to go tomorrow, but if there was one thing being around Evan had shown her it was her need to be around other people. Certainly this…*reaction*…was due to a lack of adult company. And Will needed to be around other people, too. Turning to her son, she asked, "How does that sound to you?"

"Really?" Will stared at her, barely contained excitement radiating from his little body.

"Yes, really."

"Can we go to Mellow Mushroom?"

"That sounds good to me. But first let's wash up and put on some clean clothes."

"Okay."

They were in her aging pickup truck and on their way down the drive within thirty minutes as Nellie stood forlornly on the porch. Glancing over at her son, Hannah saw the smile of boyish anticipation on his face and blessed Evan Graham for reminding her that spending time with Will having fun together was as important as anything else she could do that day.

She was almost scared to acknowledge to herself that the only thing that could have possibly made their trip into town better would have been to have Evan along with them.

Next time, Hannah thought, touching her fingertips to the place where his hand had brushed gently against her face—and surprising herself with the certainty that there would be a next time one day soon—he would be there to join them then.

Chapter Six

Evan exited off the freeway, following signs that directed him into the business district of downtown Asheville. His resentment at having to meet with Randall James personally had steadily increased on the long drive from Hannah's house. If Randall wanted Evan to do the job he'd been hired to do effectively then he couldn't be summoning him away at every whim.

Pulling into the first available space in the parking garage attached to the building where the man had his office, Evan had to take several deep, calming breaths. After all, Randall was his client, and he was also a man used to giving orders and getting his own way.

Mel had only been able to put him off for so long before he insisted on being given a progress report by

Evan himself, not by telephone, but in person. Against his will, Evan had been forced to add to the list of lies that he'd told Hannah—either intentionally or by omission—since his first meeting with her on Monday.

There had been no way around it, though. He had to meet with Randall James to keep the man happy. Otherwise Randall would have fired him and hired someone else to do his bidding. Not that Evan would have minded, but with a child's well-being at stake, Evan vowed to see the job through.

Then, of course, there was his unexpected response to Hannah.

As agreed, Evan presented himself in the expensively and extravagantly decorated reception area that opened into Randall's office suite at exactly four o'clock. The highly polished, thin-lipped young woman seated behind the antique rosewood desk eyed him with a mixture of puzzlement and admonition.

Her gaze traveled down the length of his work-stained jeans to his dirt-encrusted boots, planted firmly on the Oriental rug covering the gleaming oak floor. The last time he'd paid a visit to Randall James, he had worn a classically tailored suit and polished leather Italian loafers.

Finally she looked at the appointment book spread open on her desk, then up at him again.

"Mr. Graham, is it?" she asked, her voice polite but very chilly.

"Yes, ma'am. I'm here to see Mr. James."

"I'll let him know that you've arrived."

No offer for him to have a seat on one of the richly upholstered chairs as he'd been given on his previous foray there. Likely she didn't want to risk having to explain any damage to the fabric that contact with his work clothes might do. He was tempted to plant himself obstinately on the nearest wingback chair, but Miss Prissy was eyeing him again, as she cradled the receiver.

"Mr. James can see you immediately. Take the door to your left—"

"Thanks, but I know the way to his office. I've been here a few times already."

"Yes, of course, Mr. Graham. I believe you have."

The receptionist's smile was even colder than her tone. To Evan's way of thinking she was perfect for the position of gatekeeper to Randall James's little empire. Smiling to himself he imaged her going toe-to-toe with his own spacey but highly efficient Mel, and called it a toss-up as to which one of them would come out on top.

Evan took his own sweet time ambling down the hushed, carpeted corridor. Doors on either side were open, revealing employees still busily working despite the fact that it was a sunny Friday afternoon. James Capital Management—President and CEO Randall James—obviously had quite a bit of capital to manage.

At the far end of the corridor another highly polished but middle-aged woman, harboring her own look of disapproval, stood beside her desk, waiting to greet him.

"Ms. Matheson," Evan said, extending his hand to her.

"Mr. Graham." She, too, looked him up and down as she gave his hand a fastidiously quick, limp shake. "Mr. James is waiting."

"I'm sure he is," Evan muttered under his breath, unable to help himself or the sarcasm in his voice.

Acting as if she hadn't heard him, Ms. Matheson turned and opened the door to her employer's office.

"Mr. Graham is here to see you, sir."

"Yes, yes, and about time, too," Randall growled with obvious annoyance.

"Our appointment *was* for four o'clock, wasn't it?" Evan asked, making a point of gazing at his watch before extending his hand to the other man and adding politely, "Good to see you again, Mr. James."

Another quick handshake and Evan was directed to take a seat on one of the two truly and purposefully uncomfortable chairs across the desk from Randall. No invitation to sit on one of the small plush sofas by the expanse of windows overlooking downtown Asheville, and no offer of a drink as had been the case on his last visit there.

Fine, Evan thought, just fine and dandy. He'd dealt with uptight snobby clients like Randall James before. And true to his reputation, he'd been professional and competent every time.

"I'd expected you to have made a hell of a lot more progress with that woman by now, Mr. Graham," Randall advised, settling his bulk in the black leather chair behind his desk. He leaned back, making the springs squeak, and squinted narrowly at Evan. "I also expected you to be in touch with me *personally* on a daily basis. I don't like being put off."

The tone of the man's voice had Evan's hackles on the rise. But he took a deep breath before he spoke, reminding himself that he had to remain cool, calm and professional.

"I apologize for the slower than anticipated pace of my investigation, sir. Before I prepare my final report for you and make my recommendation on how to proceed with the matter, I want to be absolutely certain that I've covered all the bases."

"What bases?" Randall demanded, leveling his beady eyes at Evan as he drummed his fingers on the desktop. "I assumed that I'd given you all the information that you needed. How long can it take to verify that information and remove my grandson from that woman's so-called care?"

"As I explained to you at our first meeting, Mr. James, I have to have valid, documented proof that Hannah James is an abusive, unfit mother before I can begin the process of removing her child from her home. Children's Services has to be contacted about the matter, and they won't take action unless they have that proof. So far, I haven't seen any indication that Mrs. James is a danger to her son." Evan paused as Randall's eyes narrowed, then hastened to add, "But I've only been observing her for less than a week."

"And how have you been doing *that?*" the man growled, still looking unconvinced.

"I've been working for her doing day labor as a gardener."

"Ah…that must explain your…scruffy attire."

"That's also why I haven't been able to keep in touch with you on a daily basis. My cell phone doesn't work out there, and I can't afford to have her wondering why I have to go into town every day, especially since it's a two-hour-round-trip drive."

"No surprise there," Randall muttered contemptuously. "Way out at the end of nowhere—all those ignorant mountain folk holed up in shacks. Never could understand what my son saw in that woman or how he could demean himself by living in such a backward place."

Evan had to count to ten—twice—and take slow measured breaths to stop from reaching across the polished surface of the desk and pinching Randall James's fat head right off his shoulders. Hearing Hannah bad-mouthed was making him want to behave in a less-than-professional manner.

"Have you ever met Hannah or ever been to the home she shared with your son during their marriage?" he asked, his quiet tone belying the anger still simmering in his gut.

"I met her once. Had to drive all the way to Boone. Stewart insisted. I didn't know he was going to announce his engagement to the little chit. Hell, I didn't even know he'd been seeing someone seriously. There she was, plain as a poker, wearing a cheap dress and flat sandals. I couldn't imagine what my son had been thinking. I asked him, too, and he got all red in the face and told me to mind my own business. I told him he'd be crazy to marry a blatant gold digger like her when he could have any woman he wanted. I told him, too, I'd cut him off if he threw away his chance at a more lucrative marriage to someone of his own class.

"Thought he'd see that she was out for his money, but he didn't have any more sense than he had when he decided to be a college professor instead of coming to work for me. I pay for all that education for nothing. Then, he gets involved in a pointless marriage to boot. What a waste…." Randall sat forward in his chair and pounded a fist on the desktop. "But I'm not going to see my grandson go down that road."

"I understand you want the best for your grandson.

I don't know that you'll find what you're looking for on Hannah James. But like you, I want to make sure Will is in the best possible situation," he answered. "I'll do what I can to expedite my investigation."

"Good." Randall nodded once, satisfied. "Now, let's go have a couple of martinis and a big, thick steak."

Evan eyed the man with barely concealed chagrin as Randall punched the intercom button on his telephone and instructed Ms. Matheson to secure his favorite table at his favorite grossly overpriced restaurant a few blocks away from his office. Hell, he should drop this job—if for no other reason than not having to deal with Randall James again. The man could go from zero to enraged and back again faster than a speeding bullet. And he seemed to have a misguided opinion about Hannah, which Evan found extremely offensive. But it wasn't about Hannah—it was about Will. And while Evan couldn't imagine that the boy would be better off with his grandfather, it was his job—his responsibility—to make sure.

"You ready, Graham?"

Not really, Evan thought. He didn't want to spend a minute more than absolutely necessary with Randall James. Especially if it meant, as it would, that he wouldn't be able to head back to Boone immediately. But pacifying his client was part of the job, and so he said, "Whenever you are, sir," with a sigh of resignation.

"That the only outfit you got with you?" Randall demanded, eyeing him up and down disapprovingly.

"Sorry, but it is. I hadn't planned to stay in Asheville tonight. Perhaps you'd prefer that I didn't join you for dinner, after all," Evan said, trying not to sound too optimistic about that particular prospect.

"Hell, no. Who's going to say anything to you? You'll be with *me*."

Randall took his suit coat from the ornate ebony rack in the corner of his office and put it on. Then he signaled to Evan with an imperious double snap of his fingers as he headed for the door.

"Time's a wasting, Graham."

"Yes, sir, it certainly is."

With another sigh of resignation, Evan trailed after the man, already counting the interminable hours ahead of him before he could return to Hannah's house.

How could one old man consume so much food without keeling over in an excess-induced coma? Shaking his head with renewed disbelief, Evan pulled out of the parking garage in Asheville just after nine o'clock Friday night.

He had been worried that he might never get away from Randall James. But finally Evan had politely reminded Randall of his order to expedite his investigation of Hannah. Then he'd pointed out that the sooner he returned to Boone, the sooner he would have his report ready. Randall had been mollified enough by Evan's apparent devotion to duty to allow him to leave.

The drive back to Boone on mostly dark, winding roads couldn't be hurried. But that actually worked in Evan's favor. He had a chance to decompress after an unwanted evening spent in the presence of Randall James.

Evan could understand completely why Stewart James had chosen to get out from under his father's thumb. But had Stewart picked up some of his father's unpleasantness along the way?

Evan remembered how reluctant Hannah had been to talk about her husband, and how carefully she'd done so when pressed. There had been Will's comment about his father taking lots of naps, as well. He had said with a child's innocence that he and Hannah had to be quiet because waking up his father had always made him angry.

Randall had painted Hannah as the abusive one, going so far as to say that she'd allowed Stewart to die so that she could callously collect the money from his life insurance policy. Now that he'd met and spent time with her, Evan couldn't imagine Hannah doing something like that. She appeared to be one of the least grasping and acquisitive people he'd ever met.

He doubted her peacefulness and simple joy in living where and how she did could be feigned. As for using the insurance money to pay off debts or secure her property, that hadn't been the case, either.

Evan had gone into her bank and property records as well as her credit files. The house and land were hers, free and clear, just as she'd told him. She had no debts at all; hadn't for the past few years. Even the medical bills for her husband's treatment and final hospitalization had been paid off, either through the health insurance coverage he'd been provided by the university where he'd taught or by Hannah. The majority of the life insurance money had been invested for Will in a college fund, as well.

But Evan knew from past experiences that a mother's appearance wasn't everything. That the real victims—the children—could suffer without anyone ever knowing the truth. Evan's musings turned to Hannah's relationship with her husband. What kind of man had Stewart James been, and what kind of life had Hannah had with him during their marriage?

Evan had learned a little bit about the man during the few days he'd spent in Boone prior to approaching Hannah about a job. Stewart had been a tenure-track professor in the mathematics department of Appalachia State University until illness had forced him to take a leave of absence. He had been respected, yet not exactly well liked—at least just prior to his departure. Though none of the people to whom Evan had spoken could, or would, tell him exactly why.

As for the kind of life Hannah had had with her husband, Evan was at a loss. Were the shadows that lingered in her lovely eyes a result of grief alone? That would be understandable even a year after Stewart's death if they'd shared a loving relationship. But then why didn't she talk about him more freely?

Maybe it was just a matter of shyness on Hannah's part. Or maybe she had something to hide. Something about her marriage that she didn't want him to know?

The only way to find out for sure was to draw her into conversation about Stewart. Evan didn't believe that she was capable of allowing the man to die for any reason. But the accusations made by Randall James, not to mention the voracity with which he'd made them, were unsettling enough to demand a resolution as to origin and intent. Evan wanted to defend Hannah effectively against her father-in-law, but he needed to know the full story of her relationship with both Randall and Stewart James. And, of course, how Will played into all of it.

Turning at last onto the narrow, winding, mostly unpaved road that would take him after several miles to

Hannah's house, Evan was struck again by just how dark the night could be so far from even a small town. He had only driven the road in the daylight, and even though it had been raining on Monday, it hadn't been half as daunting as it was in the pitch black of the surrounding woods.

There were other houses along the road—Evan had seen them during the day. But now only an occasional pinprick of light peeping out of the dense forest growth marked their existence.

He knew he'd reached the halfway point to Hannah's property when the pack of dogs—all oversize mutts—raced down a drive into the road alongside his Jeep to challenge his presence in their territory. He had slowed down to avoid hitting any of them on his first trip up the road, but had since learned that they were savvy enough to chase him at a safe distance, snarling and barking with false bravado.

Evan almost missed the turn into Hannah's driveway. In fact, he'd driven a few yards past it, only to realize he'd gone too far. He put the Jeep in reverse, backed up slowly, then headed up the driveway, grateful to have finally made it home.

Home, he thought with a slight smile. What an interesting concept that was for him to have in connection to Hannah's house. During his childhood, home had been a scary place to be. And for most of his adulthood, home had simply been the rented space where he'd gone at night to sleep, from time to time with a woman who demanded little more of him than the occasional companionship he had to offer her.

But Hannah's house drew him in a way that was new to him. Even after only a few days, the peace and serenity he'd found there had become a desirable ingredient in his life. And so, too, had Hannah—herself the source of the very tranquility he craved.

The source of his investigation. *Stay professional, Graham,* he reminded himself. But as the house came into view and Evan saw the pale glow of light filtering through the living room windows, his spirits rose even more. He doubted that Hannah had waited up for him. But she had to have been the one to make sure that he wouldn't have to stumble around in the dark if he returned before morning.

Nellie bayed at the Jeep once, then again in a half-hearted manner from the shelter and safety of the porch. Then she trotted down the walkway to greet him as he opened the door and stepped onto the drive.

"Some watchdog you are," he chided her softly, taking a moment to pause and rub her long, silky ears.

Nellie woofed quietly in reply, took his hand in her mouth ever so gently and gave it a tug, then released him to lead the way back to the porch.

Evan entered the house and, tired as he was, it took him a few moments to realize that he wasn't alone in the living room. He had quietly closed the door after bidding Nellie a whispered good-night and started toward the staircase when he saw Hannah curled up on the sofa.

He froze halfway across the room and stared at her with surprise. Her head was cradled against a cushion and her eyes were closed. On the rug by the sofa one of her gardening books lay open to facing pages full of brightly colored flowers. She had put on dark green sweats and a pair of thick, wooly socks to ward of the nighttime chill. And for the first time since he'd known her, she had let her long dark hair fall loose around her shoulders.

Evan thought about tiptoeing quietly up the staircase, but knew he would likely wake her no matter how careful he tried to be. He didn't want to risk frightening her by creaking around the house. Nor did he want her to spend all night on the sofa when she would be much more comfortable tucked into her bed.

Then, too, there was the urge riding deep inside of him to smooth a hand over her hair, to rub a thumb along the edge of her cheekbone, to lean close to her and—

"Oh, you're home...."

Gazing at him with sleepy eyes, Hannah shifted on the sofa and pushed herself into a sitting position. Released from the immobility that had momentarily held him captive as he'd entertained a wholly improbable—and inappropriate—fantasy, Evan moved a little closer to her.

"I just came in the door, actually," he said, surprised by the huskiness he heard in his voice. "I was trying to decide how to wake you so you wouldn't end spending the night on the sofa."

"I don't usually fall that sound asleep reading. I must have been more tired than I realized...."

"You didn't finish the composting on your own, did you?" Evan asked, frowning ever so slightly.

"Oh, no," she assured him with a satisfied smile. "I followed your advice and took Will into town for the afternoon. We had pizza for lunch at his favorite restaurant, we stopped at the library to check out some books and then we caught an afternoon matinee at the movie theater. I don't know about you, but it never ceases to amaze me what Hollywood filmmakers can do with animation these days."

"A lot of it's digitally enhanced now."

"No big surprise there." Hannah yawned, then laughed softly. "Sorry about that. It's definitely not the company."

"I understand completely. I'm kind of tired myself."

"How was the rest of *your* day?"

"I've had better and I've had worse," Evan admitted with a shrug and a wry smile.

"I know what you mean."

Hannah stood, then swayed sideways as if caught by a wave of dizziness. Evan quickly stepped forward, closing the distance that remained between them, and gently put his arm around her shoulders to steady her.

"Hey, are you okay?" he asked with sudden concern.

"I'm just a little woozy, probably 'cause I'm not quite awake. Otherwise, I'm fine." She leaned against him for a long moment, belying her assertion. Then she glanced up at him, and then at the arm around her shoulder.

Evan shrugged as he released her and backed off a step or two. "Sorry."

"There's no need for you to apologize." Hannah reached out and put a conciliatory hand on his arm. "You were just trying to help."

Evan put his hand over hers and gave it a reassuring squeeze.

Her gaze softened noticeably, then she withdrew her hand and added, "I'm thinking we'd better call it a night. You had a long drive back from Charlotte."

"You're right. I did have a long drive."

Feeling guilty yet again for all the ways that he was deceiving her, Evan turned away and started toward the staircase. Any notion he'd had of sharing soft touches and sweet caresses with Hannah James had been effectively shut down by the reality of the lie he was living.

"I'll probably sleep late in the morning," she called after him as he headed up the stairs. "Do you mind if we postpone breakfast till eight-thirty?"

"Not at all," Evan replied. "That will still give me plenty of time to make up the work in the vegetable beds I wasn't able to finish today."

"See you about eight-thirty, then."

"Eight-thirty it is. Good night, Hannah."

"Good night," she said, hesitated a moment, then added softly, "And Evan…I'm glad you made it home safely."

"So am I, Hannah…so am I."

At least he could be completely honest about that particular emotion, Evan told himself when he was finally alone in his room. Unfortunately, he doubted that small grain of truth among so many lies would cut much ice with Hannah if she ever found out the real reason for his sudden appearance in her solitary life.

But then, she would only have to know if he took their relationship beyond the accepted boundaries of employer and employee. For her sake as well as his own, Evan couldn't do that—*wouldn't* do that—no matter how irresistible the temptation might be.

This was a job. That was all.

Just a job.

Chapter Seven

The favorable weather held out not only through the weekend, but also well into the middle of the following week. With the vegetable beds ready for planting by Saturday afternoon, but the little seedlings not quite hearty enough to withstand a drastic and all-too-possible drop in temperature, Hannah decided they would next focus their attention on the flower beds. First, however, she suggested that they take a break on Sunday, to which Evan readily agreed.

Hannah had half expected him to head into town or even back to the city again. The drive to Charlotte wasn't all that bad, and Charlotte certainly had much more to offer him in the way of entertainment than even a place the size of Boone. Instead Evan lingered over breakfast Sunday morning as if he had nothing better to do, giving Hannah just the spur she needed to ask if he'd be interested in taking a walk with her and Will, and of course, Nellie, too.

Evan eagerly accepted her invitation, giving Hannah the impression he'd been hoping all along that they could spend some non-work-related time together. He helped her prepare a picnic lunch to take along with them and even offered to carry the day pack for her.

Together they spent the afternoon hiking the various trails and remnants of old logging roads that crisscrossed her property. Hannah was glad that Evan seemed to enjoy the simple pleasure of walking through the cool, quiet woodland surrounding her home as much as she did. She had spent so much time tending to Stewart that all of her friends had drifted away. Now she realized how much she'd missed the companionship two adults could share.

She was also gratified by Evan's interest in the wild things growing all around them. She answered his questions about berry bushes just beginning to flower and trees in various stages of leafing out depending on the altitude. She also shared his delight at noting the occasional sign that a rabbit or a deer had traveled the same route they were on.

Stewart had never been quite as inquisitive about the flora and fauna existing with them on Hannah's mountain. Not that he'd minded living in the country. To the contrary, he'd actually craved the peace and quiet of their home after long days spent interacting with students and faculty at the university. He had often said that their home was his sanctuary and the love they'd shared his source of solace.

But he'd also been involved with his books and his computer and the latest mathematical problems he'd set for himself to solve. Nor had he ever been resentful of the time Hannah took to work in her gardens and walk with Will—at least not until the tumor-induced paranoia began to lure his brilliant mind into a dark and twisted place.

At the crest of the mountain stood a small clearing filled with short, sweet-smelling grass just beginning to reach for the springtime sun. There, Hannah suggested they eat lunch and rest awhile before heading back to the house.

Together, she and Evan spread out the small tarp she'd added to the day pack he'd carried. Then they divvied up meatloaf sandwiches, corn chips, molasses cookies and cartons of apple juice she'd had on hand for just such an occasion.

Hannah had even remembered to add a handful of dog biscuits to keep Nellie happy. Luckily a drink for the dog wasn't necessary. Three spring-fed creeks ran in different directions nearby and Nellie was more than happy to stand in the icy water and slurp to her heart's content.

"Eating the way I've been it's a good thing I'm also getting lots of exercise," Evan said as he polished off the last of his second sandwich with obvious relish.

"You're probably eating more because you're getting more exercise," Hannah pointed out. "The fresh air can really stir up one's appetite, too."

"It's energizing in a lot of ways, isn't it?"

"It is as long as it's also cool. Once the temperature starts to climb and the humidity begins to build, I predict we'll be moving a lot slower."

"I have to agree with that."

Tilting her face to the warming rays of the sun, Hannah smiled as a drift of cool breeze teased the tendrils of hair escaping from her braid. She hadn't had such an enjoyable walk in a long time, and she had an idea it was Evan's company that had added the heretofore-missing ingredient to the whole experience.

Much as she had always liked walking with Will and Nellie, it wasn't quite the same as having another adult along, as well. Especially an adult like Evan Graham.

Last night she had welcomed the arm he'd slipped around her shoulders to steady her when she'd been hit by an unexpected wave of dizziness. But he had been out late, and she didn't know where. And while she didn't comment on it, she caught the scent of alcohol on his breath. The possibility that he might not be completely sober had stirred myriad unpleasant memories from the not-too-distant past.

To battle against the pain in his head, Stewart had taken to drinking more whiskey than was good for him. And when he'd been drinking, he'd become, by turns, either angry or amorous. She'd had no choice but to appease him as best she could, if for no other reason than to keep herself and Will safe from his potentially violent rages.

"You're looking rather somber all of a sudden," Evan commented, drawing her back to the moment at hand. "I hope it wasn't something I said."

"No, not at all," Hannah assured him with a quick glance in his direction. Then, turning her attention to Will, playing fetch with Nellie a short distance away, she added, "I was just thinking about days past."

"Not particularly good thoughts?" he asked, stretching out his legs on the tarp and settling back on his elbows.

Hannah hesitated for an instant, half wanting to confide in him about the last awful months—*years,* actually—of her marriage. But she was equally determined to hide the truth about just how badly she'd allowed herself to be treated by a man who could have given Dr. Jekyll and Mr. Hyde a run for his money.

Pride won out in the end. The past was over and done. She'd made her choices and she'd lived the consequences. In the end, after she'd learned of the tumor eating away at her husband's brain, she had known she'd done the right thing, standing by him. Now, almost a year later, she didn't want or need Evan Graham's pity.

"Mostly just sad thoughts," she answered at last, forcing herself to meet his gaze, eyes steady, and smile. "But it's too nice a day for those, isn't it?"

"Thoughts about your husband?" Evan prodded, unsettling her not only with his probing look, but also by pressing the issue after she had signaled her desire to see it closed.

"Surely that's understandable, isn't it?" she countered with a question of her own.

Unwilling to give away any of her true feelings on the matter of Stewart, Hannah subtly shifted her position on the tarp, turning her back to Evan. All that had happened between her and her husband—as a result of his illness, she now knew—was better left in the past. Even if the pain of the experience lingered deep within her.

"Was he a good husband to you, Hannah? Did he take care of you and Will? Did he make you happy?"

Startled by the edge of intensity she heard in Evan's voice, Hannah glanced over her shoulder at him. He eyed her without apology as she frowned at him in dismay, unable to hide completely her consternation.

"Yes…yes, of course," she said.

Barely resisting the urge to tell him point-blank that it was really none of his business, Hannah scrambled to her feet and called out to Will.

"Time to head back to the house, sweetie," she called. "We don't want to risk getting caught in the dark."

"Okay, Mommy."

"Do you want to finish your juice so I can stash the carton in the day pack?"

"Yes, please."

As Will ambled in their direction, one arm thrown affectionately around Nellie's neck, Evan stood, too, and put a conciliatory hand on Hannah's arm for just a moment.

"Hey, I'm sorry. I was out of line there," he said. "I had no right poking around in your private business, especially when it's obvious that you're still grieving."

"It's all right," she replied, still without looking at him. "I understand your curiosity, but I'd really rather not talk about my husband."

"Then I'll consider the subject closed." Again Evan touched her arm lightly, and added as Will joined them, "Want to help me fold up the tarp?"

"Yes, of course."

After handing her son his carton of juice, Hannah bent and grabbed an edge of the tarp. Together she and Evan folded it into a neat square that fit easily inside the day pack.

The walk back to the house naturally took less time since it was all downhill. They didn't pause, either, to admire the scenery or to inspect more closely any of the plants along the way that they'd failed to notice on their way up the mountain.

Hannah had no idea how Evan felt, but she was suddenly ready for some private time. The questions he'd asked her about Stewart and their marriage had upset her even more than she'd first realized. She had resisted responding aloud, but the answers still lingered in her mind.

Was he a good husband to you, Hannah? Not for a long time.... Did he take care of you and Will? No, I took care of him while Will learned to stay out of the way.... Did he make you happy? For a while, and then he scared me half to death....

In the year that had passed since Stewart's death Hannah had studiously avoided dwelling on the frightening days, weeks, *months* she had lived through prior to the diagnosis of his brain tumor. She couldn't change what had happened to him or to their marriage. But neither could she convince herself, no matter how many times she tried, that she hadn't somehow been responsible for his behavior toward her and Will.

Yes, Stewart's physical illness had made him mentally ill, as well. Still, there had to have been something she could have done to save him from himself.

The sun had begun to dip behind the treetops by the time they arrived back at the house. Hannah offered to warm up the remainder of a chicken casserole she'd served for dinner earlier in the week, but much to her relief, Evan made an excuse about having to go into town on an errand.

He seemed to sense her grim mood as well as the reason for it, and she was grateful that he acted accordingly without any further prompting. Sitting across the kitchen table from him, attempting to make small talk, would have been almost more than she could tolerate that particular evening.

After Evan took off for town, Hannah and Will ate dinner together in front of the television set—a rare treat guaranteed to garner complete cooperation from her young son when she announced a slightly earlier-than-usual bedtime for him that night. Halfway through the story he'd insisted that she read before lights-out, he was soundly asleep.

Alone in the kitchen, Hannah tidied up. Then she poured a glass of wine—a rare treat for herself—slipped into her jacket, went out on the porch and sat on the old wooden swing.

The air had gone from cool to cold and smelled faintly of wood smoke from the fire she'd lit in the Franklin stove. The single lamp she'd left on in the living room provided the only light—a soft, warm glow visible through the windows. In the night quiet she could hear the spring-fed creek babbling just beyond the driveway, and occasionally the rustle of some creature in the undergrowth.

Eventually Nellie clumped up the porch steps to snuffle and wag a greeting. Then she heaved herself onto the swing beside Hannah, rested her head on Hannah's thigh and sighed with canine contentment.

Hannah wished that she could relax even half so simply and so easily. But even with the mellowing influence of a single glass of rich red wine, tension still tightened her muscles and her mind refused to settle.

Memories of the hurt, the fear and the humiliation she'd suffered at Stewart's whim, stirred by Evan's questions, flitted and danced across the surface of her thoughts. And no matter how she tried, she couldn't seem to shove them back into the imaginary box she'd created for them. Instead, they taunted her with *should* have and *could* have and *would* have as if she'd actually had a choice.

Hannah couldn't fault Evan for his curiosity. Her own open, friendly nature, not to mention the loneliness that made his companionship so welcome, had been the real culprits. Had she behaved toward him more as an employer than a chum, surely he wouldn't have felt so free to probe her past or her personal life. But he had been, and was, so likeable and so good-natured. It had been so easy to feel comfortable enough with him to let down her guard more than usual. As for her physical response to him…well, that was best left avoided altogether.

At least he had finally taken heed of her resistance to his interrogation, though. He had retreated to his own corner, so to speak, and had allowed her to do the same. She was grateful, of course, but gratitude alone wouldn't prevent a similar episode from happening again.

Starting tomorrow she would have to establish some new and more stringent boundaries between them. She could, and would, continue to be cordial toward him, but without giving the impression that certain…liberties would also be allowed.

The crunch of tires on the gravel driveway coupled with the dog's leap off the swing signaled that Evan had returned from town. Swallowing the last of her wine, Hannah slipped off the swing, as well, and quickly made her way into the house.

She didn't want him to think she'd been waiting for him even though she knew in her heart that to a certain extent she had been. Bad enough that he had caught her at it last night. A second time, especially after their exchange that afternoon, would be too much.

Hannah was safely in her bedroom with the door closed by the time she heard Evan's slow, measured tread on the staircase. He must be tired, too, she thought, or surely he would have moved more quickly. Unless he was hoping she would hear him and come out to talk awhile.

Even after all the mental gyrations she'd gone through the past couple of hours, she was tempted. Luckily, though, she wasn't tempted quite enough.

To Hannah's relief, Evan honored her hopefully subtle attempt to reestablish a little more employer-employee distance between them Monday morning. She welcomed him into the kitchen for breakfast with a friendly greeting. But she didn't ask him about his trip to town or, for that matter, anything else of a personal nature. He, in turn, asked only about her plans for their workday, making no reference at all to the previous day's tension between them.

As they began the laborious task of weeding the flower beds, Evan seemed honestly interested in learning to recognize the various perennials fighting for space in the grossly overgrown garden plots. Fortunately, he was a quick study, noting without too much trouble the differences between those plants meant to be growing in the beds and those that weren't. He also welcomed her direction and didn't hesitate to ask an appropriate question whenever he wasn't sure how to proceed.

Clearing the flower gardens of unwanted weeds and debris was even more physically demanding than clearing the vegetable gardens had been because the work had to be done on hands and knees, one small patch of ground after another. Otherwise too many desirable plants would also be destroyed. For the same reason, the job was also extremely tedious and time-consuming.

Even with Evan's conscientious help, Hannah was all but overwhelmed by the breadth of the undertaking she'd set for them. Almost two years of inattention had resulted in a huge mess to be cleaned up. Had it not been for the richness of the soil, the regularity of the rainfall and the basic hardiness of her perennials, she wouldn't have had any foundation at all for the growing season ahead.

As it was, Hannah found—most notably—violets, primroses, sweet woodruff, apple-scented and wild geraniums, iris and English bluebells and forget-me-nots, all starting to display foliage, stretching skyward and greening up fast. With the addition of a little compost and a continuation of warm, sunny days interspersed with an occasional slow, soaking rain shower, she should have a wealth of flowering plants ready to sell at the first farmers' market in early May.

Amazingly the weather held through Wednesday, allowing her and Evan, and Will, too, to make a sizable dent in all the work that had to be completed. Evenings, after dinner and when the dishes were done, Evan retired to his room. During the workday it was difficult enough for Hannah to avoid relaxing into the easier camaraderie they'd shared the previous week. So she was grateful for that courtesy, as well.

At least she told herself that she was grateful—or should be—as she sat alone on the sofa, trying to read, after she'd tucked Will into bed. Ignoring the weight of loneliness that had once again settled deep in her soul took a huge amount of effort, though.

She hadn't realized how much she'd craved the subtle closeness she'd begun to share with Evan until she'd found it necessary to either draw away from him or talk honestly about the past. She had thought that revealing all to him about her marriage would be too painful, not to mention too embarrassing to bear. But it hurt, as well, to cut herself off emotionally from the friendship and the understanding he had seemed to want to offer her in exchange.

Thursday dawned dark and dreary with a cold rain falling steadily. Hannah's major concern was that the temperature might also drop significantly, threatening to ice over and freeze the young plants still hardening up on the deck. The weather forecast on the local radio station promised a low only in the midforties, however, making it unnecessary for them to embark on the miserable job of moving the plants back into the greenhouses.

Instead they were able to spend the morning and early afternoon in one of the greenhouses planting seeds in peat pots to start the annuals Hannah would sell in late May and early June. There were a lot of local people who wanted touches of summer color in their flower beds without all the work of nursing seeds into seedlings.

Confined more closely with Evan in the narrow aisles of the greenhouse, Hannah couldn't seem to help brushing up against him occasionally with her hand or her arm. In fact, each time it happened, she thought all the more about it happening again. And the more she thought about it happening again, the more it seemed to happen, until her face burned with embarrassment and her hands shook with agitation.

To his credit, Evan didn't seem to notice at all. Either that or he wasn't the least bit disconcerted by the physical contact imposed on them by their immediate and unavoidable proximity. As had been her dilemma the past few days, Hannah wasn't sure if she was glad or sad that he was so obviously immune to her... charms.

Finally about three o'clock she'd had enough. Since it was also time to get Will up from his afternoon nap, she announced her intention to go back to the house and start a pot of homemade soup for dinner.

"You're welcome to quit early, too," she said to Evan. "Especially since we've run out of peat pots and it's too nasty out to drive into town to get some more."

"I can use the time to work on your Web site," he said. "I've been thinking about how best to set it up the past few evenings, but that's about all I've had the energy to do."

"That would be really nice," Hannah replied as she washed her hands at the sink in the greenhouse.

She didn't add that she was also relieved that he'd be busy upstairs, giving her a chance to regain some of her lost composure while she started dinner.

Will was just waking up from his nap as they walked into the house, and unusually for him, he wasn't exactly

in the best of moods. He stood in the living room looking like a little lost soul, his dark hair spiked up and his
eyes bleary. He even clutched a small faded blue blan-
ket in one hand, a sure sign that all wasn't right with his
world.

As Evan looked on from the doorway, Hannah hurried over to her son and touched maternal fingertips
first to his forehead, then to his slightly flushed cheek.
He suffered her attention with a wobbly frown that
spoke of tears likely on the way.

"Hey, cutie," she said after a moment, smoothing a
hand over his hair, relieved that he wasn't running a
fever. "How about some milk and cookies?"

"Don't want milk," he said in an aggrieved tone.
"Want apple juice."

"Okay, apple juice it is," she answered agreeably.
"How about a cookie, too?"

"Chocolate chip."

"I only have oatmeal cookies left in the tin."

"Chocolate chip, chocolate chip, *chocolate chip,*"
Will demanded.

Hannah drew a deep, calming breath, bracing herself for a possible temper tantrum. This was the last
thing she needed after a day of hard work. Before she
could tell Will again that she had only oatmeal cookies on offer, however, Evan stepped forward and spoke
directly to him in a teasing voice.

"I know how you feel, buddy. I was hankering after
one of your mom's chocolate chip cookies myself. But
you know her oatmeal cookies are pretty darn good,
too. Why don't we have them today, and then maybe
she'll make some chocolate chip cookies for us tomorrow?" He flashed a conspiratorial look at Hannah,

then glanced back at Will again. "How about that deal, Mom?"

"Sounds like one I'll be more than able to keep," she replied with an appreciative smile.

"Will?" Evan prompted when her son still seemed to be considering his choices.

"Uh…okay." He pouted. "But I want to play *Candyland*, too."

Hannah saw her opportunity to get a pot of soup started, then relax awhile quickly fade away. One game of *Candyland* could, and often did, take hours. And with Will in such a prickly frame of mind, he could easily end up in tears if she refused to play with him.

Again, Evan came to her rescue, this time in a truly kind and generous manner.

"Hey, Will, what a good idea. I haven't played *Candyland* in years, but I seem to remember it was lots of fun," he said.

Will's expression brightened considerably as he gazed at Evan.

"You *like* to play *Candyland*?"

"Oh, yeah, I like to play *Candyland*."

Hannah couldn't help shooting Evan a disbelieving look. But she was savvy enough to acknowledge the warning glance he sent her way and keep the "Oh, really?" comment she'd been about to make strictly to herself.

"What about you, Mommy? Are you going to play, too?" Will asked, his tone no longer quite so querulous.

"I'm going to start chopping vegetables for a pot of beef-and-barley soup. How does that sound for dinner tonight?"

"Mmm, that sounds good," her son replied. Then to

Evan he added as he headed for the kitchen, "We have to eat our cookies before we can get out the game board."

As Evan moved to follow Will, Hannah stepped forward and put a hand on his arm, halting him for just a moment.

"Thanks for running interference for me," she said, keeping her voice low.

"My pleasure," he replied with a slight smile.

"Obviously you haven't played *Candyland* in a very long time, especially with a competitive five-year-old boy," Hannah said, her own smile just a tad on the wry side.

"Actually, I don't think I've ever played *Candyland* at all."

"Oh, wow—then you're in for a real treat."

Hannah couldn't help shooting him a sympathetic look despite her teasing tone.

"It's that bad, huh?" Evan asked, obviously no longer sure of exactly what he'd gotten into.

"I wouldn't use the word *bad*. But I'd definitely fortify myself with oatmeal cookies if I were you."

She gave his arm another appreciative pat, then headed after Will.

With Evan and Will settled at the kitchen table, first with cookies and milk, then the board game, Hannah sliced and diced onions, carrots and celery for her pot of soup. She then put a little olive oil in a pan and browned cubes of beef along with the vegetables, filling the kitchen with a mouthwatering aroma that had Evan commenting enthusiastically.

The rain continued to tap against the windows with a soft, steady beat that acted as a pleasant counterpoint to the classical music she'd tuned in to on the radio. Much like gardening, cooking had always filled Hannah with a sense of contentment and that Thursday afternoon was no different for her.

At least it wasn't until the large glass measuring cup filled with water somehow slipped from her hand and crashed to the floor halfway between the sink and the pot on the stove into which she'd already dumped the meat and veggies.

Hannah wasn't sure why she froze in terror, her wide-eyed gaze fixed on Evan. It had been over a year since Stewart had last screamed at her for being careless, and Evan hadn't once displayed anger in her house.

But his questions Sunday afternoon had brought memories of Stewart and his erratic behavior closer to the surface of her mind than they had been in a very long time.

Evan stood and started toward her wordlessly and Hannah took a step back, trying, unsuccessfully, not to flinch as Will jumped up and ran, sobbing, to her side.

"Hey, it's okay," Evan said, his voice soft and soothing. "It's only a little water spilled on the floor. The measuring cup isn't even broken. Let me get some paper towels and help you clean it up."

"You're right. It's only a little water on the floor," Hannah agreed.

Meeting his sympathetic, yet questioning gaze, she forced herself to smile. Then she knelt to comfort her son as Evan grabbed the roll of paper towels on the counter and began to mop up the floor.

Chapter Eight

Though Hannah did her best to make light of the incident once she had soothed away Will's tears, Evan couldn't dismiss the undercurrent of fear he'd sensed in both mother and son when he'd stood so abruptly from the table. Naturally, he had been startled by the crash of the measuring cup on the floor. Still, his only intention had been to help with the cleanup.

But the panicky way in which Hannah and Will had looked at him had spoken volumes about what they'd expected of him instead—some sort of tirade or, at the very least, a harangue. No matter that he hadn't had the right to respond angrily to such a small and insignificant accident. After all, he was merely a guest in Hannah's house.

Yet it seemed that in their minds he had been

equated with someone who had not only assumed that right, but had also exercised it often enough to leave indelible marks on their souls. And Stewart James was the only one Evan could think of who'd had the necessary combination of close proximity and questionable personality to cause such lasting trepidation in Hannah and her young son.

"Really, I could have done that," Hannah said as he tossed a wad of wet paper towels in the trash can, then unrolled a couple more sheets to give the floor a final swipe. "I *should* have done it since I'm the one who made the mess."

"Like I said, it's just a little water on the floor. It's no big deal, and it's all mopped up now," Evan replied. "Anyway, Will needed you more than the floor did a few minutes ago." He hunkered down in front of the boy and chucked him gently on the chin. "All better now, buddy?"

"Yes, sir."

Will shot him a sheepish smile as Hannah used a tissue to wipe the last of his tears from him cheeks.

"How about you, Mom?"

Evan looked at Hannah as he stood again.

"Yes, thanks. I'm fine, too." She blushed as she met his gaze, then quickly looked away. "Sorry to have been so…rattled over such a silly thing."

"Happens to all of us at one time or another," Evan assured her. "Something someone else sees as a minor mishap can seem like a major catastrophe to us."

"Or vice versa," Hannah murmured, still without looking at him.

"Or vice versa," Evan repeated, acknowledging his understanding of all that she'd left unsaid the only way he could—in his simple, straightforward confirmation.

He had every intention of at least attempting to discuss the subject with Hannah at greater length, but not in front of Will. He couldn't just let slide the fact that she'd been afraid of him and his possible reaction to water spilled on the floor. Not even knowing that she'd likely shut down on him as she had Sunday afternoon when he'd ignored her unspoken warning signals and had probed a little too insistently into part of her past life that she'd considered none of his business.

For now, though, he focused his attention on Will.

"Ready to finish our game now?" he asked the boy.

"Yes, please."

"Then let's get busy. But first…" Evan looked to Hannah again, his smile meant to be teasing. "Why don't you tell me how much water you need in the pot?"

"Four cups should do it," she replied as she returned his smile with a slightly wry one of her own.

"Four cups, it is," he said, crossing to the counter to rinse out the measuring cup and refill it.

The remainder of the afternoon progressed without further incident. With the pot of soup bubbling on the stove, yeast rolls from the freezer thawing on the counter and the rain still falling outside the house, Hannah joined Evan and Will at the kitchen table for a second round of *Candyland*.

To Hannah's obvious relief, Will's moodiness lifted completely. And both Hannah and Will seemed relatively happy and relaxed in his presence, much to *Evan's* relief.

By dinnertime, even Will had had enough of *Candyland*. He was content to watch a favorite show on television while Evan helped Hannah with the dishes after they'd eaten. Then the two of them joined Will in the living room until the program he was watching ended and Hannah announced that it was time for him to get ready for bed.

The past few evenings, Evan had excused himself and gone up to his room after helping with the kitchen cleanup. Tonight he lingered in the living room, however, determined to talk to Hannah. He knew that he risked upsetting her as he'd done once already. But under the circumstances, he deemed it a risk well worth taking.

Had he been only mildly curious about her marriage to Stewart James, he would have likely kept his distance as he'd been doing the past several days. But his need to know was just that—a *need* that he had yet to explain to himself in a satisfactory way.

From his first meeting with Hannah, he had been attracted to her for an odd mix of reasons. She was both like and unlike the women to whom he'd been drawn in the past. She was strong and self-sufficient—traits he had always admired. Yet she wasn't demanding or impossible to please, as had been the *drama queens* he'd seemed fated to hook up with in the past.

Trying to make them happy had been as inconceivable as trying to make his alcoholic mother happy. Often left twisting in the wind, he had always felt as if he weren't quite good enough for any of them—a debilitating pattern he'd finally acknowledged and had since avoided at all cost. Eventually, he'd also given up on ever finding anyone with whom he'd be able to have a serious, long-term, committed relationship.

But Hannah James definitely wasn't a *drama queen*. She handled unsettling situations calmly. She didn't argue simply for the sake of stirring up trouble. She seemed content to live in a peaceful place and to lead a peaceful life, much as he knew he wanted to do. And rather than use his strength, his kindness and his consideration against him, she also seemed to honestly appreciate those positive traits that he embodied.

But there was a shadow lurking darkly over her effervescent spirit—a shadow that could have only been cast by her husband, and that still held her captive to whatever she'd suffered at his hands in the past.

If nothing else, Evan wanted to see Hannah finally free of that shadow once and for all. She was so courageous and so confident in so many ways. He wanted her to be equally courageous and confident in her personal relationships, as well, whether with him or with someone else after he was gone.

"Oh, hey…I thought you'd gone upstairs," Hannah said, pausing just inside the doorway of the hall that connected the two downstairs bedrooms to the living room.

"Not yet," Evan replied, unable to ignore completely her uneasiness at finding him still sitting on the sofa.

He didn't want to make her nervous—didn't want her feeling apprehensive in his presence. But neither did he want to miss the chance to talk to her about what had occurred in the kitchen that afternoon.

"Well, you're more than welcome to watch television or…whatever." She hesitated a long, uncertain moment, then added brightly, "I'm going to make some cinnamon-nut muffins for breakfast tomorrow."

As she headed for the kitchen, Evan switched off the

television set, stood and followed after her, determined not to let her put him off.

"Need some help?" he asked when she glanced back at him, a slight frown lining her forehead.

"Not really," she answered in a slightly truculent tone. Then, seeming to realize how ungracious she must have sounded to him, she added as she turned away again, "Unless you want to oil the muffin tins."

"Sure, I'd be happy to do that for you."

Wordlessly, Hannah took two tins from a cabinet and set them on the kitchen table along with a can of shortening. Then as Evan washed his hands at the sink she assembled bowl, wooden spoon and ingredients on the counter and began to mix the batter.

Sitting at the table, Evan carefully applied shortening to the tins as he gathered his thoughts. He was only going to have this one opportunity to draw Hannah out about her husband. He didn't want to botch it up by coming on too strong. But neither did he consider a teasing tone to be appropriate. Finally, he settled on simple yet nonconfrontational honesty about how her behavior had affected him as the best way to broach the touchy subject.

"Please tell me if I'm wrong, but when you dropped the measuring cup full of water on the floor this afternoon you, and Will, too, seemed a little…afraid of how I'd react. I hope I haven't given either one of you any reason to feel frightened of me when we're together."

As Evan had fully suspected would happen, Hannah not only stopped stirring the batter for the muffins, but also tensed noticeably before he'd even finished speaking. She neither turned to look at him, nor answered him immediately, making him wonder how truthful her response would be, if, indeed, she made one at all, aside from telling him to mind his own business.

"Of course you haven't given us any reason to feel frightened when we're together," Hannah said at last, still keeping her back to him. "You've worked hard and you've been a perfect gentleman. I wouldn't have let you stay with us otherwise."

"But you were afraid of how I'd react earlier, weren't you?" Evan prodded gently. "Can you tell me why that was? *Will* you tell me, please? Because I really hate distressing you in any way or for any reason."

Hannah glanced back at him, then away again, giving him time only to see something akin to embarrassment in her dark eyes. Then she shrugged as if trying to make light of the subject.

"Force of habit, actually," she began in a self-deprecating tone. "It was foolish of me to be so careless with the measuring cup. It could have shattered into a thousand pieces on the floor and cut any one of us."

"It was an *accident*—" Evan said.

"A *foolish* accident," Hannah cut in. "The kind of accident that my husband couldn't tolerate. He wasn't the type to suffer foolish behavior lightly, and after he became ill, he had a bit of a temper. If he'd been sitting at the table this afternoon, he would have been angry with me, and it would have been my fault for not paying attention to what I was doing."

"But Stewart wasn't sitting at the table today," Evan pointed out, carrying the muffin tins to the counter, then moving to the sink to wash his hands again. "And you didn't drop the measuring cup on purpose. It was an accident, and accidents happen all the time without anyone getting angry. I'd say anyone who could get so upset as to frighten his wife and son about something so minor had a serious problem with anger management—especially anyone who blamed his reaction on anyone but himself."

"I understand all that, but when you've been foolish on a regular basis, no matter what the reason for it, it's really hard not to begin to believe—"

Coming up beside Hannah, Evan gently put his hands on her shoulders and turned her to face him, unable to allow her to demean herself any further. Startled, she looked up at him, tears glittering in her eyes, her pain and humiliation so obvious that his heart ached for her.

"You are not a fool, Hannah James. You have never been one and you never will be, no matter how your husband behaved toward you. You are a strong, vibrant, loving woman. You had to be in order to raise your son to be a happy, healthy child, and also to survive here on your own not only through your husband's illness, but also during the past year, without falling to pieces. Stewart was the real fool for not appreciating you the way you deserved."

"He was ill," Hannah said, looking away as she tried, unsuccessfully, to blink away her tears.

"I'm sorry about that, Hannah, truly sorry. But even knowing that he was ill doesn't make what he did any easier to bear, does it?"

"No...no, it doesn't."

As if released from a great weight by her admission, Hannah finally gave in to her tears and began to cry in earnest. His heart aching all the more for her, Evan gathered her into his arms and held her close, smoothing a hand over her hair and letting her weep.

The storm of emotions had obviously been building in her for a very long time, and he waited patiently for it to blow itself out. At the same time, he savored the solid feel of her body close to his, long and lithe and as strong as her spirit.

Evan knew that he had no right to be thinking sexual thoughts about Hannah James—not then, not ever. He was living in her house under false pretenses. Within a few days, another week at the most, he would have to go back to Charlotte, back to his real life, whatever *that* meant. Because right here, right now, holding Hannah in his arms felt more damn *real* to him than anything else he'd experienced in years.

He had thought about it, yearned for it—hell, he had even *dreamed* about it so intensely that he'd awakened once already—hot and hard and ready to claim her as his own. And no amount of lecturing himself about the impossibility of building a lasting relationship on a foundation of lies and deceit had curtailed his desire.

"I am *so* sorry," Hannah murmured as her sobs finally began to subside. Her hands resting on his chest, she took a tentative step back, then looked up at him. Her cheeks were still damp with her tears, but the shadows in her dark eyes seemed to have lifted. Attempting a slight, apologetic smile, she added after a moment, "I didn't mean to lose control like that."

"I'd say it was about time you did," Evan replied. "Feel better now?"

She eyed him thoughtfully for several seconds, then nodded once in agreement.

"Yes…yes, I *do* feel better…much better."

"*Good.*"

Intending only to give her a chaste, compassionate kiss on the forehead, Evan pulled her close again. But somewhere between intention and the act of touching his lips to her brow, the need that had been riding deep inside of him for so many days took on a life of its own.

The startled-fawn look in her eyes as she gazed up at him with quiet surprise melted the last of Evan's reserve, as well. Instead of letting her go, turning away with an excuse and taking himself off to bed, he pulled her even closer. Then he bent his head and claimed her mouth with the fierce and ardent abandon of a man claiming his mate.

Fleetingly, and much too late, he thought that such an advance might frighten Hannah half to death. But her response to him was equally sudden and pleasantly, reassuringly surprising.

She neither protested nor made an attempt to pull away from him. With a naturalness that spoke of true emotions, she slid her arms around his neck, tilted her head just so and kissed him back.

Gratified by the honesty of her ardor, Evan teased at her mouth with his lips and tongue, then sighed with exquisite delight when she opened up to him even more completely. He was on the verge of moving his hands from the small of her back to her breasts when a belated warning bell went off in his head.

What the hell was he doing, not only kissing Hannah James, but also getting ready to touch her intimately as a prelude to taking her into his bed? What did he have to offer her but the eventual revelation of lies told? He couldn't go any further with her—in fact, he had already gone much too far.

NO POSTAGE
NECESSARY
IF MAILED
IN THE
UNITED STATES

BUSINESS REPLY MAIL
FIRST-CLASS MAIL   PERMIT NO. 717-003   BUFFALO, NY

POSTAGE WILL BE PAID BY ADDRESSEE

SILHOUETTE READER SERVICE
3010 WALDEN AVE
PO BOX 1867
BUFFALO NY 14240-9952

Get FREE BOOKS and a FREE GIFT when you play the...

LAS VEGAS
GAME

*Just scratch off
the gold box with a coin.
Then check below to see
the gifts you get!*

YES! I have scratched off the gold box. Please send me my **2 FREE BOOKS** and **gift for which I qualify.** I understand that I am under no obligation to purchase any books as explained on the back of this card.

335 SDL D7ZH   235 SDL D7Y7

FIRST NAME

LAST NAME

ADDRESS

APT.#

CITY

(S-SE-06/05)

STATE/PROV.

ZIP/POSTAL CODE

7	7	7	Worth TWO FREE BOOKS plus a BONUS Mystery Gift!
🍒	🍒	🍒	Worth TWO FREE BOOKS!
🔔	🔔	☘	TRY AGAIN!

www.eHarlequin.com

With no small amount of regret, Evan broke off their kiss and took a decisive step away from her. Dreamy-eyed, Hannah gazed up at him wordlessly, her luscious mouth a damp and slightly swollen testament to the passion they'd just shared.

So captivating did she appear that Evan almost pulled her into his arms again, almost relinquished what little self-control he had remaining. It was only the knowledge that if he stopped now then certain disclosures about himself would never have to be made that held him firm.

"That was totally, completely out of line, Hannah," he said, giving her shoulders a squeeze, then shoving his hands into the back pockets of his jeans. "I hope you'll accept my apology and my promise that it won't happen again."

Still eyeing him in silence, Hannah frowned in obvious confusion. Slowly she touched her fingertips to her lips as a blush spread across her cheeks. Then she blinked once and gave her head a shake as if to clear it.

"There's...there's no need to apologize, Evan," she said at last, lowering her gaze as she turned back to the counter. "I know you meant well and certainly there hasn't been any harm done."

He had meant a hell of a lot more than *well,* but telling her so was out of the question. As for harm done—he was glad she was relatively unscathed by their kiss, but his heart was damn sore at the moment.

"Thanks for being so understanding, and as I said, it won't happen again."

"Yes, well, I did get that message."

For a long moment, she glanced back at him, the

hurt in her eyes undeniable. Then she busied herself stirring the muffin batter again.

Much as Evan despised himself for causing her such unnecessary pain, he held tight to the reins of his potentially runaway emotions. A little disappointment now was a hell of a lot better than the damage that could be done to her if they became more intimately involved and then she discovered the truth about him and his relationship to Randall James. A relationship he had reevaluated a thousand times since meeting Hannah.

"Is there anything else I can help you with tonight?" he asked, aware of how diffident his tone had become.

"Oh, no," she answered with the merest edge of sarcasm, still not looking at him. "You've helped quite enough already, thank you very much."

"Well, then, I'll head upstairs to bed."

Not what he wanted to say, but rather what he had to say to spare her any more hurt.

"Good night."

"Good night, Hannah."

Evan hesitated for another indecisive moment, but Hannah continued to ignore him as she began to fill the cups in the muffin tin. Finally, he turned and walked away.

Alone upstairs, Evan logged on to the Internet and answered a couple of e-mails from Mel—neither urgent enough to warrant a trip to Charlotte, much to his relief. Then he tried to read for a while without success.

He wished he could take a long, solitary walk, but the rain, falling harder than ever, kept him captive in his room. More than once he had to stop himself from pacing like a caged beast, not wanting to disturb Hannah with the creaking of floorboards caused by his measured footsteps.

A hot shower did little to relax him, and finally, for want of anything better to do, Evan crawled into bed and switched off the lamp. Lying in the pitch-dark, he realized that the odds of his actually falling asleep that night were zero to none. He hadn't used nearly enough physical energy during that rainy indoor day to stop his mind from racing, and the trails his thoughts wanted to take led down roads he knew he shouldn't be traveling.

Any reminiscing about the kiss he'd shared with Hannah was strictly off-limits. But keeping his mind from wandering in that direction meant that he had to focus on something else instead. In desperation, he went over the little Hannah had finally told him about her husband.

Now that he knew Stewart had been abusive toward Hannah, Evan could understand more completely why she'd given his father a wide berth after his death. She'd had a hard enough time coping with Stewart's behavior. She must have known instinctively that Randall would beat her down even more. Since she hadn't owed her father-in-law the same allegiance that she'd believed she'd owed her husband, she had wisely refused to knuckle under to his demands despite the fact that Randall could have helped her financially.

Evan found himself wondering, too, whether Stewart's hurtful behavior had actually been caused by his illness. Hannah had obviously convinced herself that his bad temper was strictly the result of the brain tumor that had eventually killed him. But Hannah had a generous heart. Nor had she spent enough time with Randall to realize that Stewart could very well have been predisposed to the same hot flashes of anger as his father, given just the right trigger.

None of that really mattered much now, though. Evan had seen enough of Randall in action and had spent enough time with Hannah and Will to know that Will had been and always would be safer, more secure, more deeply loved and cared for by his mother than by a bitter, angry, resentful old man. And he now had all the information he needed to report as much to Randall James.

He also had all the information he needed to feel completely comfortable resigning from the case. He would even strongly advise the man to leave Hannah alone—she was completely innocent of the accusations Randall had made. Then, his job done, he could go back to Charlotte almost immediately.

Only that would leave Hannah without the help she needed to finish her garden prep.

Of course, he could always hire someone to help her himself. He could vet the man personally and pay him extra on the side to keep a special lookout for further trouble from her father-in-law. He had done something similar in a few cases he'd been hired to handle in the past.

But Evan couldn't quite bring himself to do it with Hannah. Not because he'd have a hard time finding someone he could trust. That would actually be quite easy. The hard part for Evan was taking himself out of Hannah's life—taking himself away from her soft smiles, her sweet laughter, her warm and gentle nature…and most importantly, the chance to share with her one last loving, passionate kiss.

Yet he couldn't risk Randall sending someone else to continue the investigation who might blow Evan's cover.

With a low groan, Evan sat up and punched his pillow with a vicious fist—once, twice, three times for good measure. Then he flopped down again and stared into the darkness, cursing not only the choices he had but also his inability to make the one he knew he should.

Chapter Nine

Hannah wasn't sure if she was more embarrassed or angered by the way her exchange with Evan had concluded earlier that evening. She only knew that she couldn't stop thinking about it, and the longer she replayed the scene in her mind, the longer she went without sleep.

He had initiated all that had happened between them—beginning to end. She now realized that he had followed her into the kitchen intentionally, not, as she'd originally thought, because he'd lacked anything else better to do.

He had meant to broach the subject of her irrational response to a very minor accident all along. And more than likely, he'd only waited until Will was tucked into bed because he had known, quite rightly, that there were some things about her husband and her marriage that she would never discuss in front of her son.

Listening to the incessant rain drum against her bedroom windows, Hannah wondered if she should have told Evan the little she had, regardless of whether Will had been present. Too late now, of course—she couldn't take back the admissions she'd made.

She had thought earlier that she owed Evan some explanation of her behavior. Her fearfulness toward him, as well as Will's, had been completely undeserved, not to mention truly unfair. He had been upset by it, and justifiably so. He had given her no cause to be afraid of him in the ten days they had lived and worked together, and he'd had a right to be reassured of that fact by her.

But had she said too much by way of explanation? Had she revealed more about Stewart and her marriage than had been absolutely necessary under the circumstances? Had she given him too large a glimpse at the anguish she'd suffered before Stewart finally died? And, in doing so, had she stirred such pity in Evan Graham that he had deemed it necessary to kiss away her tears as if she were a child?

As yet another hot flush suffused Hannah's face she tossed aside her bedcovers, slipped out of her bed and paced to a window that looked out into darkness. She pressed her forehead to the cold glass and squeezed her eyes shut, hoping without much hope to negate the memory of how Evan had taken her in his arms and kissed her almost senseless.

She was sure that at first he'd only meant to comfort her. But then she had clung to him, had opened her mouth to him so eagerly that he'd finally had to pull away from her as if extricating himself from a cling-ing vine.

Stunned as she had been his kiss, she had been even more stunned by her response to it. She hadn't thought sexual desire would ever be a part of her repertoire of emotions again. Not after the awful nights she'd spent silently submitting to Stewart's harsh, often hurtful de-mands.

But Stewart had been a tender, considerate lover once. Evidently her need for that kind of closeness, that kind of gentle, caring intimacy with a man hadn't died com-pletely.

Only Evan hadn't been opening the door to a ro-mantic liaison between them. He had merely been giv-ing her a little added comfort to go along with the shoulder upon which he'd so kindly allowed her to cry. She had been the one to take their kiss a step further— a step that was actually further than he'd intended to go.

He had backed off with a determination too appar-ent for her to ignore, adding for good measure—in case she hadn't quite gotten the message—that kissing her would never happen again. He had said that *he* was out of line, taking the blame upon himself for *her* lasciv-ious behavior. But Hannah knew now, as she'd known then, that *she* had been the one to assume too much, and to move beyond the bounds of common decency.

She wanted to believe that if her emotions hadn't been running quite so high, she would have never al-lowed the kiss in the first place. But alone in her bed-room, with dawn only a few hours away, Hannah couldn't be anything but honest with herself.

She knew that if Evan came to her again at that

very moment, if he pulled her close and kissed her in the same way, she would kiss him right back again, just as fiercely and with just as much need as she'd done in the kitchen that evening.

Because if he kissed her again after saying so succinctly that he wouldn't, it would be no accident then. It would be with absolute and undeniable intent.

Finally trailing back to her bed, Hannah wondered if Evan was as wide-awake as she. She doubted it sincerely. What did he have to toss and turn about, after all? He had admitted to making a mistake and he'd also apologized for it. And she had been quick to reassure him that she'd taken no offense.

He had probably been sleeping peacefully for hours already, while she continued to tie herself into overly emotional knots about something she couldn't have changed…even if she wanted to.

Amazingly, the rain had let up by the time Hannah's alarm clock went off at seven the next morning. She had slept at last, but only for a couple of hours—just long enough to leave her feeling distinctly out of sorts. The damp chill in the air and the lingering low gray clouds didn't help her mood much, either. Nor did Will's rambunctious behavior or Evan's polite reserve. Although, in all honesty, the way she was feeling, nothing anyone said or did that Friday morning would have pleased her.

Taking the easy way out with Will, Hannah allowed him to eat his cereal in front of the television set. Unfortunately, dealing with Evan wasn't quite so simple.

If he noticed her disagreeable disposition, he was wise enough not to comment on it. He joined her in the kitchen at seven-thirty sharp, shaved and showered and dressed for outdoor work, wished her a good morning, then helped himself to coffee and a muffin.

As she rooted around in the freezer, searching for the packet of chicken breasts she wanted to bake for dinner that night, he ate in silence. Not up to casual conversation, she tried to ignore him. But the spicy tang of his aftershave drifted on the gust of heat coming from the Franklin stove. There was also no avoiding the thoughtful glint in his bright blue eyes as he watched her move from the refrigerator to the sink, icy packet of chicken finally in hand.

"Unless the rain starts up again, we can go back to weeding the flower beds this morning," Hannah said, determined to get past their first awkward minutes together as best she could. "It's going to be really muddy out there, but the weeds will be a lot easier to pull with the ground so wet."

"We should be able to make up for the time we lost yesterday, then," Evan replied.

"Yes, we should," Hannah agreed, setting the packet of chicken on a plate to thaw.

Evan's chair scraped on the floor as he stood from the table. Hannah expected him to cross to the coffeemaker to refill his mug. Instead he came up right behind her and put a hand on her shoulder. Startled, she whipped around to face him. His hand dropped away, but he stood his ground, almost, but not quite, crowding her against the sink as he met her wide-eyed gaze intently.

"When I apologized for kissing you last night it wasn't because I found it unpleasant or distasteful in any way—quite the contrary, in fact. I only apologized because I felt that I'd crossed a line with you that wasn't appropriate without an invitation. I didn't want to frighten you or cause you concern in any way. Neither did I want to leave you with the impression that I found you unattractive, because, again, quite the opposite is true."

As had happened the night before, Hannah felt her face flush, but this time it was for an altogether different reason. Rather than suffering from embarrassment, she experienced both a sense of satisfaction and—surprisingly—no small measure of delight.

The sincerity with which Evan had spoken, coupled with the straight-on, unflinching look he gave her, convinced Hannah that what he'd said was true—and that he hadn't said it because he'd felt he had to. He hadn't owed her any explanation for his behavior aside from the perfectly acceptable one he'd given her already. That he had taken the time to clear up the misconceptions he must have known she'd had said a lot about the kind of man he was.

Suddenly the weariness in her soul drifted away and the dreariness of the day mattered to her not at all. Meeting Evan's gaze, Hannah smiled for the first time that morning and saw, at once, how the worried look on his face disappeared completely.

"I didn't find it unpleasant, either," she admitted shyly. "But I guess I made that kind of obvious to you last night."

"In the most gratifying way possible," he acknowledged, touching a hand to her cheek as he smiled back at her. "I didn't want you to think I was taking advantage of you, though, or that I was forcing myself on you at a moment when you already seemed to be in a sensitive state of mind."

"And here I've been thinking that I was the one who had taken advantage of you by mistaking your kindness and understanding for something more."

"We're some pair, aren't we?"

"Too considerate for our own good, at least in some situations—if that's possible," Hannah said, her smile turning wry.

"Considerate is a good thing to be, and you definitely have me beat on that particular score," Evan replied.

"I'm not so sure that's true. In fact, I was about to say the same for you, Mr. Graham."

"Nothing like a little friendly competition in the modesty department to keep things interesting, is there, Mrs. James?" Evan's tone was teasing, but then he added more seriously, "You are a special lady, Hannah. Don't ever forget it, no matter what happens."

Again he touched her face with his hand, this time gently brushing his knuckles along the line of her jaw. The tenderness of his touch coupled with the compliment he'd given her warmed Hannah, heart and soul. The renewed intensity of his gaze sparked anew the deeper longing that had gripped her the night before, as well. She leaned closer to him and put her hand on his chest, her eyes locked with his.

"You, too, Evan," she murmured softly.

Then, sensing his intent as he bent his head, she parted her lips ever so slightly in delicate anticipation.

"I shouldn't do this," he muttered, his mouth mere inches from hers.

"Oh, yes…you should…" Hannah replied, encouraging him with a soft smile.

"What are you doing, Mommy?" Will demanded

from less that two feet away, his voice filled with lively curiosity.

Hannah wasn't sure if she or Evan was the one most startled. She did know that when she jumped back the top of her head soundly smacked the tip of his chin, causing both of them to utter a surprised "oh." Laughing self-consciously, they stepped apart and focused their attention on her son.

"Um, I'm just talking to Evan…um, Mr. Graham." Willing away the hot flush suffusing her face, Hannah moved past Evan and crossed to where Will stood, empty bowl in hand. "Looks like you've finished your cereal."

"Yes, Mommy. May I please have a muffin now?"

"Yes, you most certainly may."

Relieved that her son had accepted her explanation so easily, Hannah took his bowl from him, put it in the sink, then put one of the freshly baked muffins on a plate for him. Her heart stopped racing and her hands shook only a little. Still, she didn't dare look at Evan as he lounged against the counter, now holding a steaming mug of coffee.

"Thanks, Mommy," Will said, taking the plate in both hands.

"Do you want more milk, too?"

"No, thank you." He turned away, took a few steps, then paused and glanced back at her with wide, innocently angelic eyes. "Mommy, were you *kissing* Mr. Graham?"

"Um…no…no, I wasn't, Will," Hannah said, her face burning all over again as Evan gave a muffled snort of laughter.

"'Cause it's okay with me if you do," her son added, smiling at her beneficently.

"Well, I'll be sure to keep that in mind if the… um…occasion ever arises," she assured him.

"Are we going to weed the flower beds today?"

"Yes, we are. We can get started just as soon as you finish your muffin."

"Okay, Mommy."

As Will headed back to the living room, Hannah sensed Evan's gaze on her. She tossed a quick glance at him and saw him grinning wickedly.

"Talk about getting caught in the act," he said, his voice low.

"*Almost* caught in the act," Hannah muttered primly, crossing back to the sink.

"I don't think he would have minded." Evan took her by the arm and turned her gently so that she faced him again. "Now the question is—would you?"

Hannah meant to be firm with him—meant to remind him that Will was only a child and they really should watch how they behaved together when he was nearby. But her convictions melted away under the laser heat of his crystal-blue gaze.

How could she deny that she'd wanted him to kiss her—wanted it badly before Will interrupted them? That would be a terrible lie especially for someone as honest as she had always tried to be.

"No, I wouldn't have minded at all," Hannah admitted at last without any further wavering.

"I can't tell you how good that makes me feel," Evan replied, then drew her closer. "But I can certainly show you…."

His kiss had a gentle, claiming quality to it. There was no hurry as he put his mouth on hers, no urgency to make the moment seem stolen or unseemly. With a thoroughness that took Hannah's breath away, he tasted her, using his lips, his teeth, his tongue, his pleasure in her response not only uninhibited, but also undisguised.

Hannah couldn't have helped herself if she tried. The fresh scent of soap and aftershave clinging to his skin, the dark taste of cinnamon and coffee on his mouth, and the hard line of his muscular body all teased at her feminine senses, inviting her long-dormant desire to come out and play. She sighed softly, angling her head to give him easier access.

Then as gently as he'd begun the kiss, Evan ended it. Raising his head, he looked deep into her eyes and rubbed a thumb along her cheekbone.

"If that was too forward of me, please say so," he urged.

"Not at all," Hannah answered a little breathlessly.

"Mommy, I'm done with my muffin."

Once again Will interrupted them, bouncing into the kitchen with his empty plate. Reluctantly Hannah moved away from Evan, first sending a glance his way. Then she turned back to the sink to wash up their breakfast dishes.

"Why don't you and Mr. Graham go outside and get started where we left off on Wednesday afternoon? I'll be out to help you as soon as I do a few things here in the house."

"Sounds good to me," Evan agreed. "How about you, buddy?"

"Me, too, Mr. Graham," Will said. "Can I splash in the puddles if I put on my rubber boots, Mommy?"

"I suppose so." To Evan she added as Will dashed off, "Do you mind helping him—?"

"Splash in the puddles? I'd be delighted."

He grinned at her, making her laugh out loud.

"You didn't let me finish," she chided him. "I meant help him on with his boots."

"Oh, sure. I'll do that, too."

He saluted her smartly, then went off to find her son.

Alone in the kitchen, Hannah realized she was smiling quite foolishly. Though what could be simple-minded or featherbrained about feeling so good she certainly didn't know. She had as much right as anybody to be happy and being happy about a kiss from Evan Graham wasn't doing anybody any harm. More than that, it was actually doing *her* quite a lot of good.

Stewart had done a fine job of battering her self-confidence. But Stewart was gone now, through no fault of hers. With him Hannah also wanted gone the influence he'd once had over her feelings about her herself and her desirability as a woman.

As Evan had pointed out, her husband's behavior toward her might not have been completely his fault, but that knowledge didn't make the memory of it hurt any less. But dwelling on those memories when she could focus on all the positives of the present moment was as unnecessary as it was unhealthy. Evan saw her as she'd seen herself before Stewart had turned on her in anger and in pain, and Hannah was more than ready to also see herself that way again.

There was something else Hannah wanted to do, too—something she had done to a very small degree last night. She wanted to tell Evan the whole truth about her six-year marriage to Stewart James. She wanted him to know how her husband's illness had affected all of them, including Will, and that the scars he'd left on her soul were only now starting to heal.

But she had been so weak and so afraid during the last year of Stewart's life—a fact she couldn't hide from Evan. So many times she had thought of taking Will away with her, but fear of the unknown had held her fast. How would that revelation of her cowardly behavior affect his high regard for her?

Having no acceptable answer to her question, Hannah set it aside as she finally joined Evan and Will in the garden area behind the house.

Her prediction that the ground would be saturated from all the rain had been right on target. Weeding was much easier, of course, but also a whole heck of a lot messier. Though it wasn't actually raining anymore, there was a fine mist in the air that clung to everything, making their work damper and chillier than Hannah would have liked.

Since she didn't want any of them coming down with a cold, she insisted that they take a longer-than-usual lunch break. They savored big bowls of hot homemade vegetable soup while their boots and coats had a chance to dry out in front of the Franklin stove she had kept fired up in the kitchen for the past few days.

Will wasn't much interested in taking a nap and re-calling his cranky mood the previous day, Hannah allowed him to go back outside with them in the afternoon. He spent more time playing with Nellie—splashing with the dog in puddles or chasing her up and down the driveway—than actually pulling weeds. But he was happy and that, in turn, made Hannah happy, too.

On the other hand, Evan had seemed to become quieter and a little more withdrawn as the day progressed. The easy banter they'd exchanged at first soon petered out. And having Will with them at lunch had made the chance for anything but the most casual conversation unlikely.

Hannah began to wonder if perhaps Evan had found a reason to regret the exchange they'd had that morning in the kitchen. But the times she sensed his gaze on her as they worked within a few feet of each other that afternoon, and glanced his way, he returned her questioning look with a soft, seemingly wistful smile. Her doubts would be temporarily chased away, only to eventually creep up on her again, unbidden.

Maybe he was tired, too, she thought when she suggested about four o'clock that they call it a day and he readily agreed. Glancing at him surreptitiously, she noted a definite sag to his shoulders and a weariness in his normally dancing, devilish eyes.

Maybe she hadn't been the only one unable to sleep last night. That possibility really shouldn't make her feel better, but it did. She would much rather that his silence be a product of fatigue than self-reproach.

Lining up his boots and coat by the Franklin Stove Evan leant truth to her theory.

"Do you need help with dinner?" he asked.

"Thanks for the offer, but I'm keeping it simple tonight," she said as she positioned another chair by the stove and hung Will's coat over the back of it to dry. "Baked chicken and a broccoli-rice casserole that's ready to go from the freezer into the oven, too."

"Sounds really good." He smiled in the wistful way she'd noted earlier, then added, "I think I'll go upstairs and take a shower, unless there's something else you need for me to do."

"Nothing I can think of," Hannah replied, though she caught herself longing for another kiss just like the one he'd given her that morning. "Dinner should be ready at five-thirty."

"I'll be down then."

Hannah longed to take a shower, too. But Will was looking a little too sleepy to leave on his own in front of the television set. She didn't want him dozing off now—he'd want to stay up past his normal bedtime later and she wasn't up to handling that.

She enlisted his help drying off Nellie so the dog could come inside for the night. Then she had him set the table and finally played several hands of *Go Fish* with him until it was time to eat.

Evan didn't appear to be much revived by his shower, and Hannah and Will drooped even more than he did over dinner. They were all hungry enough to enjoy the hot meal, but they did so mostly in weary silence. With just a few bites left on his plate, Will put his head down on the table and closed his eyes, much to Evan and Hannah's amusement.

"I hate to say it, but I'm with him," Evan admitted with humor.

"So am I," Hannah agreed, scooting back her chair. "If you don't mind, I'm going to take him to his room and tuck him into bed."

"Then I'll take care of storing the leftovers and cleaning up the kitchen," Evan said as he, too, stood from the table.

For once Hannah resisted her natural urge to tell him not to bother.

"Thanks," she said instead. "That would really be great."

"You look like you could use a hot shower and an early bedtime, too."

"You're right about that."

"How about if I turn out the lights down here when I'm done in the kitchen? Then you can head straight to bed yourself."

"That sounds great, too."

Hannah smiled up at him as she gathered Will into her arms. The sleeping boy sighed and snuggled against her without opening his eyes.

"Did you have anything special planned for tomorrow?" Evan continued as he began to stack their plates.

"I need to go into Boone to buy groceries and stock up on more peat pots at the gardening center." She hesitated a moment, then added shyly, "You're welcome to come with us if you'd like. Although I know it's Saturday and I promised you weekends off and I'll understand completely if you have—"

"I'd like to go into Boone with you and Will tomorrow, Hannah," Evan said, halting her runaway ramble with his clear and steady gaze. "In fact, I can't think of anything I'd enjoy more."

Mentally cursing the hot flush that suffused her face yet again in his presence, Hannah looked down at Will, still sleeping in her arms, then back at Evan again.

"I'd like it, too," she admitted, meeting his gaze in an equally steady way.

There was no sense pretending anything else. Having Evan Graham in her life meant more to her every day they were together. He had brought with him not only the end of loneliness, but also the first promise of contentment in the companionship of another.

"What time should I be ready to go?"

"If we leave about eight o'clock, we can stop at Rosie's Café for breakfast. She makes the best waffles and apple fritters in the county. It will be my treat, too," she said.

"Oh, no, it's going to my treat, Mrs. James," Evan countered sternly. "Consider it a small payback for all the wonderful meals you've served the past two weeks."

"Well, if you insist...." She smiled at him gratefully.

"I absolutely do."

In Hannah's arms, Will stirred and whimpered in his sleep.

"I'd better get this boy into bed," she said, finally turning away. "Thanks again for taking care of the cleanup."

"My pleasure, Hannah," Evan replied, his low voice making the simple words sound almost sexy.

Glancing over her shoulder, Hannah saw the wistful look in his eyes and wondered again at the reason for it. What was it that Evan Graham wanted but seemed to think he couldn't have?

Maybe she would find out tomorrow. Though, on second thought, as she eased Will out of his clothes and into his pajamas, she wasn't sure she really wanted to know.

She much preferred to enjoy Evan's company, no questions asked, at least for the time being. He had signed on to help her for the summer, and they still had a lot of work to do in the gardens.

There would be more than enough opportunities to

get to know him better in the days ahead. And there would also be more than enough opportunities to find out if her feelings for him were the real thing, or just the response of a lonely woman to the first available man who'd happened to come along.

Chapter Ten

As he climbed the staircase to his room, Hannah's house calm and dark and quiet all around him, Evan knew he was playing with fire. But he couldn't seem to stop himself. Honestly and truthfully, he'd had no intention of kissing Hannah again that morning. He couldn't say it had just happened, either.

He had seen the look on her face as she'd bustled from the refrigerator to the sink, doing her best to ignore him. Recalling their conversation the previous evening, he had suddenly realized that the words he'd said—meant to reassure her—had apparently come out sounding callous and insensitive to her ears.

Evan had been anxious to right that wrong. But in so doing he had dug himself in even deeper, simply by speaking the truth. Hannah's sweet forgiveness, coupled, as it had been, with honest admissions on her own, had drawn him to her all over again, like a bee to clover honey. He had tried to resist the urges pounding in his blood, but Hannah's allure had been just too much for him. She had wanted another kiss as much as he and she hadn't been afraid to let him know it.

There were so many things Evan had wanted, but never had, so many things he had accepted long ago that he would likely never have no matter how deeply he yearned. He hadn't wanted one last kiss from Hannah James to be counted on that melancholy list.

Of course, the only way their kiss in the kitchen that morning could be counted as a *last* one was if he packed up and left town first thing the following day, Evan reminded himself. As he stripped out of his clothes, pulled on a pair of sweatpants and climbed into bed, he knew he had no more intention of doing that than he had of flying to the moon.

In fact, he planned to spend the entire weekend ahead with Hannah and Will, enjoying their company as much as he could while the specter of Randall James lurked in the back of his mind.

There had been an urgent e-mail from Mel waiting for him when he'd logged on to the Internet after taking his shower. Apparently Randall had demanded that Evan present himself in Asheville as soon as possible for another personal audience.

Evan had fired back a response to Mel before going downstairs for dinner, asking her to assure the man that he would be in touch early next week. Before he could log off, Mel had replied that she'd done as requested.

She also warned that if Randall's tone had been any indication, there would probably be hell to pay.

Evan was more than willing to take that risk. Randall James was a liar and a bully, and Evan was more than capable of putting him in his place. Actually, he was looking forward to it, but not until after he'd had one more weekend with Hannah and her son.

Sleep came a little more easily to Evan than it had the previous night. The cold, damp weather coupled with a full day of hard physical labor made stretching out under a pile of quilts on a comfortable bed a luxuriously relaxing experience. He didn't have to try nearly as hard to shut down his mind. But with sleep came dreams of Hannah, vivid yet all too fleeting, that had him awakening just after dawn, eager for the day to begin.

After only a small argument about who should do the driving, the three of them left Hannah's house at eight o'clock, as planned, with Evan at the wheel of his Jeep. On the porch, Nellie bayed unhappily at being left home alone, but the poor dog would have been even more upset at being locked in the Jeep while they ran their errands in town.

Low gray clouds scudded across the sky, promising off-and-on waves of showers to come, but that didn't dampen their spirits in the least. Evan was especially glad to see that Hannah looked much more rested than she had the previous day as she added to the items on her grocery list. Will sat on the backseat, contentedly paging one last time through the storybooks that they would return to the library later in the day.

Just like any other happy family heading out on a Saturday morning to run errands and shop, Evan thought with a mix of satisfaction and sadness. There was nowhere else on earth that he would rather be than driving down the narrow, winding North Carolina mountain road to Boone with Hannah and Will. Yet no matter how hard he tried to pretend otherwise, he knew these moments with them were only temporary and, all too soon, would be over forever.

"Rosie's Café first?" he asked, determined not to let his mind wander too far beyond the next few hours.

"Yes, please," Will called out from the backseat. "I'm *so* hungry and Rosie makes the *best* waffles in the whole world."

"If that's okay with you?" Hannah asked, looking up from her list with a teasing smile.

"Far be it from me to deny a hungry boy his favorite waffles," Evan replied. "Just be sure to tell me when and where to turn."

"It's just north of town, about a mile or so down a side road. I'll let you know way ahead to time when to start looking for the turnoff."

"You're my kind of navigator," Evan said, his smile widening with appreciation.

"I try my best."

With a slight shrug of her shoulders, Hannah looked away.

"And you succeed...beautifully."

Taking a hand off the steering wheel, Evan gave her arm a gentle, reassuring squeeze.

"Thanks."

She glanced at him again, her dark eyes sparkling anew with feminine pleasure.

"You're very welcome."

Rosie's waffles were as delicious as Will had said

they'd be—served up hot off the waffle iron with slabs of smoked ham and real maple syrup. Customers came and went as they ate, keeping the place lively and full of people. Most of them were locals and almost all nodded and said a friendly hello to Hannah and Will.

To Evan they directed curious but kindly gazes, making him feel that any friend of Hannah's would also be considered a friend of theirs. Evan quickly realized, as well, that she was held in high regard by all who knew her. But then, that came as no surprise to him.

Over Hannah's objections he picked up the check when they were ready to go.

"But I just paid you," she said. "You should use the money for yourself."

"There's nothing I want or need right now except the pleasure of your company," he assured her quite truthfully. "You've also cooked for me the past two weeks. You deserve a treat today. I'd like to be the one to provide it for you."

"Well, then, thank you very much," Hannah replied, blushing in the pretty way she did whenever someone or something caught her slightly off guard.

They headed off to their next stop at the city library where Will chose several new storybooks to replace the ones he was returning. A puppet show was about to begin in the children's room and they stayed for that, as well.

Hannah urged Evan to use the hour for himself, but again, he reminded her that he'd rather stay with her and Will than take off on his own. Surprisingly, he enjoyed the puppets more than he'd expected. They were cute and silly, and the dual-level story suitably entertained the adults as well as the children.

As he laughed along with Hannah and Will, Evan again experienced a sense of family—a sense of being an important part of a very special whole. He was filled with a warmth of spirit he'd rarely experienced in the past, and certainly not in his own unhappy childhood. The life Hannah had made for her son was a good life, and for that above all else, he admired her.

By the time they were ready to leave the library, the sun was peeking out from behind the clouds, announcing a temporary respite in the rain showers. They decided to drive across town immediately to the huge outdoor garden center so Hannah could replenish the supplies they'd used during the past few weeks.

She also wanted to stock up on the organic fertilizers and insect repellents she would soon need, as well. Managing pests in the gardens was a challenge, Hannah advised rather ruefully. But she believed it was worth the extra effort to protect her environment from chemical contamination as much as she possibly could.

Amazingly, it was nearly one o'clock by the time they finished at the garden center. Not so amazingly, they were all hungry again. The rain was also threatening to return with a vengeance. Hannah prevailed in treating them all to a Mellow Mushroom pizza piled high with veggies and Italian sausage. They still had grocery shopping to do, and both Hannah and Evan agreed on the importance of embarking on that adventure with a full stomach.

The grocery store Hannah favored was crowded with customers that Saturday afternoon. To save time and also to keep Will entertained, she gave half her list to Evan and sent him off with her son as if on a scavenger hunt for cereal, canned goods and cleaning supplies.

Since Evan hadn't a clue as to how the store was laid out, it really was a matter of searching for the necessary items while Hannah waited to be served at the deli and the meat counters.

On his own, Evan also chose a couple bottles of wine and a couple pounds of gourmet coffee as his special contribution. He would have been happy to buy more, but he didn't want to upset or embarrass Hannah. He had realized that she was prickly about paying her way, and he respected that about her. She was also considerate of his financial situation, or rather what she believed to be his financial situation. He didn't want to make her suspicious by spending more than she'd believe he was able to afford.

They were all standing together in one of several long lines at the checkout counters when a woman with a little girl about Will's age maneuvered her cart into line right behind them.

"Mommy, look," Will said, tugging on Hannah's hand and pointing to the pair. "It's Mrs. Dietrich and Molly."

Hannah glanced back curiously and at the same moment, the woman smiled with genuine warmth.

"Hannah James?" she said. "I haven't seen you in, well…it has to be almost two years. How are you…and Will, too?"

"Fine, thanks," Hannah replied, turning to face the short, middle-aged woman with dark curly hair more fully. "It's nice to see you again, too, Essie. How about you and your family—I hope you're all doing well, too."

"Very well." Essie Dietrich seemed to hesitate, then added politely, "I was sorry to hear about your husband. I know you had a…difficult time with him during his…illness."

Evan noted how carefully the woman chose her words, her glance darting to Will who had angled into a position where he and Molly could more easily eye each other. There was nothing intentionally rude, hurtful or intrusive about her comment. Rather, she seemed quite sympathetic, making it obvious to Evan that she hadn't much cared for Stewart James or his behavior toward Hannah.

"The card you sent after the funeral meant a lot to me." Hannah smiled graciously, belying the faint flush that suddenly stained her lovely face, signaling her discomfort. Then she gestured to Evan, neatly changing the subject by including him in their conversation. "By the way, this is Evan Graham. He's been helping me get my gardens ready for the growing season. I'm hoping to have a stall at the farmers' market again this spring and summer." Turning to Evan, she added with a bright smile, "Evan, this is Essie Dietrich. She's the principal at the elementary school where I used to teach. Will is starting kindergarten there in the fall."

"Nice to meet you, Mrs. Dietrich," Evan said, extending his hand to her.

Essie eyed him with interest, her handshake firm and businesslike.

"Nice to meet you, too, Mr. Graham," she said. "I can't tell you what good news it is to hear that Hannah will finally be offering her plants and produce for sale at the farmers' market again. Her produce is outstanding and her perennials have to be the healthiest and most luxurious ones I've ever planted in my flower beds."

"Thanks, Essie. I really appreciate the compliments," Hannah said, her blush now one of pleasure.

"Now all we have to do is get you back in the classroom. She was one of my best teachers, Mr. Graham. I had hoped she'd come back to work again last fall. In fact, I believe I said as much in the card I sent."

"Yes, well, it was a little soon after…after Stewart…." Hannah demurred.

"I understand," Essie assured her. "But it's been almost a year now, and I've just found out I'm going to need a third-grade teacher in September. Milly Hargrave has finally decided to retire. She and her husband want to move to Florida. The job could be yours if you're interested."

Hannah eyed Essie with surprise for several seconds. Evan thought she would turn down the offer, but finally she smiled and nodded her head.

"I *am* interested, Essie, *very* interested."

"That's wonderful, Hannah," Essie replied with an equally wide smile. "Come in to see me one afternoon next week. We can talk more then and perhaps get started on the necessary paperwork."

"Are you going to teach at my school?" Will asked, gazing up his mother with wonder in his eyes.

"We'll see, Will. I have to talk to Mrs. Dietrich first."

"Oh, Hannah, having you at Elmwood Elementary School again would be a real delight," Essie said. "We've all missed you so much."

"Thanks, Essie—thanks so much. I'll see you next week, then," Hannah assured her as Evan finally wheeled their cart up to the checkout counter.

Watching Hannah as they waited for the groceries

to be scanned and put into paper sacks, Evan noted a subtle difference in her overall demeanor. She stood a little taller and she glowed with a new measure of self-confidence.

By practically offering Hannah a job at her elementary school based mainly on past performance, Essie Dietrich had spurred her into taking another giant step on the road to making a new life for herself and her son. And by agreeing to take a job that would bring her into closer contact with the world outside the safe haven of her mountain home, Hannah had proven herself more than ready for whatever challenges lay ahead.

Though he still didn't know the whole story of her marriage to Stewart James, Evan had a good enough idea to understand just how far Hannah had come since his death. And any worries he'd once had that Randall James would mow over her with his bullyboy tactics now seemed unnecessary. She was capable of standing up to the man on her own. But he had also seen that she had at least one friend around town to guarantee that she would never have to do it alone.

Again Evan was forced to face the fact that most, if not all, of his original reasons for remaining in Boone no longer existed. But again, he also resisted paying heed to the warning bell clanging in his head that cautioned him to either leave town as soon as possible or come clean with Hannah about his motive for showing up on her doorstep in the first place.

Talk about being caught between a rock and hard place....

"Well, that was a nice surprise," Hannah said when

they were back in the Jeep again, the groceries stored alongside the gardening supplies. "And timely, too, since I've been thinking about going back to teaching again now that Will will be starting school."

"She seemed really pleased that you were interested in a job. You must have impressed her with your teaching skills," Evan replied as he pulled out of the parking lot onto the main drag that would take them back through town to the highway and home.

"I only taught for a few years before Will came along, but I really loved my job and I loved all the kids, too."

"Even the bratty ones?"

"Even the bratty ones," Hannah admitted with a laugh.

"I'm not going to be bratty at school," Will said proudly from his place on the backseat.

"That's good to hear," Evan said as Hannah turned and smiled at her son. "You tend to miss a lot of really important things when you're busy behaving badly."

"I couldn't have said that any better myself," Hannah acknowledged, shooting Evan an appreciative glance.

"Is the school very far from where you live?" he asked.

"It's actually only about twelve miles from the house. But it takes at least twenty-five or thirty minutes to get there because you can't drive much over twenty-five miles per hour on the mountain road, and that's in good weather. Luckily the school district factors in extra days to make up for the times we have to take off for foul weather. A heavy snowfall can make it impossible for most folks to travel, so we just stay put until the roads are plowed."

"I hadn't thought about driving this road after a snowstorm," Evan admitted as he guided the Jeep around a blind curve. "You must feel really isolated then."

"Not really. I grew up out here, remember? And come the end of January or the beginning of February, it's nice to have a good excuse to spend a few days at home instead of standing in front of a classroom full of antsy kids."

"I hadn't thought of it that way, but I can definitely see your point."

By the time they pulled up in front of the house, the gray day had turned into a dark, rainy evening. Nellie greeted them with a round of joyous barking, but wisely didn't venture off the porch.

Hannah opted to leave the gardening supplies in the back of the Jeep rather than get wet hauling the stuff back to the greenhouses and the shed. Unloading the groceries couldn't wait, but with the three of them working together, they managed to get all the bags inside the house in only two trips back and forth. At Evan's insistence, they all worked together to put things away, as well, making short work of a job that he knew Hannah would have found tedious on her own.

"I suppose we're all hungry again," she said, holding open the refrigerator door and staring at the various containers of leftovers arranged on the shelves. "I can heat up the last of the vegetable soup, if anyone's interested."

"I can open a bottle of wine, too," Evan offered.

"I don't want soup," Will said, the long, busy day starting to affect his temperament. "I want peanut butter and jelly."

"Then that's what you'll have," Hannah replied. "Followed by a bath and bedtime."

Will groused a bit more, but ate his sandwich while Hannah put the soup on the stove to simmer. Then he took a quick bath, put on his pajamas, climbed into bed and was sound asleep before Hannah got to the third page of the story he'd wanted her to read.

On his own in the kitchen, Evan set the table, opened the bottle of red wine he'd bought at the store and stirred the soup until Hannah joined him again. He thought she might be as tired as her son as a result of all the running around town they'd done. But as she took a sip of the wine he'd poured for her, she looked amazingly rested and relaxed.

"Mmm, that's very good," she said.

"It's a favorite of mine," Evan replied. "I'm glad you like it, too. Have a seat and I'll serve the soup."

"Thanks."

Hannah sat at the table and watched as Evan ladled the hot soup into the bowls he'd set out earlier. The rain seemed to have let up again, so the only sound in the kitchen as they began to eat was the pop and crackle of the wood he'd added to the Franklin stove.

"I had a really good time today," Evan said after they'd had a chance to take the edge off their hunger.

"So did I," Hannah agreed, sending a soft smile his way.

"Are you still feeling good about the job Essie Dietrich mentioned?"

"Oh, yes, very good. But also very surprised," Hannah admitted, looking away as she toyed with the stem of her wineglass. "Essie tried to get me to come back to work last year, but I just wasn't ready. Lately

I'd been wondering if maybe I'd blown my chance of ever teaching at Elmwood again by turning her down. I've been thinking that I'd like to go back to teaching in the fall, but it would have been difficult to teach at one school and have Will attending classes at another one."

"That definitely doesn't seem to be the case. Essie Dietrich obviously thinks very highly of you, Hannah."

Evan stood and picked up their empty bowls, then crossed to the sink.

"Even after all the years I've been out of touch," Hannah added in a bemused tone.

"She didn't seem to mind," Evan said, then hesitated as he turned to face her again. "Besides, you obviously loved teaching, and I've seen for myself how much you love your gardens, too. But you let it all go. You're such a strong and vibrant woman, Hannah. What caused you to give up those things that meant so much to you?"

Hannah looked back at him, her dark eyes troubled. Evan waited for her to make some flimsy excuse or, even worse, to tell him that he should mind his own business.

Instead, after several long silent seconds, she said quite simply, "It's a long story, one I've mostly kept to myself. I'm not sure talking about it now will do any good."

"Maybe talking about it would be the best way to be rid of the hold it still seems to have over you," Evan suggested gently.

"Yes, you're probably right," she agreed with a soft, sad smile. "But are you sure you want to be the one to hear it?"

"Only if you're sure you want to tell me, Hannah."

"Yes...yes, I believe I do," she said after a moment more.

She took a deep breath and prepared herself to begin.

Chapter Eleven

"Would you feel more comfortable if we sat in the living room?" Evan asked, showing Hannah the same consideration that he had shown her from the first.

She wasn't sure she'd be comfortable talking about her marriage to Stewart James anywhere, but she *would* prefer to be out from under the glare of the kitchen's fluorescent light.

"Yes," she said, then shot Evan a wry smile. "I wouldn't refuse another glass of wine, either."

"Nor would I."

He smiled, too, as he topped off their glasses, set the now empty bottle back on the counter and flipped the switch that turned out the kitchen light.

"Come on," he said, offering her his hand when she still hesitated at the table.

Hannah wondered if Evan had any idea what a huge step she was about to take, then realized that it didn't really matter. The step was hers, and hers alone, to take...or not. Doing so would only be for her benefit.

She also wondered if she'd be able to go the whole distance and tell Evan everything, and again she knew that it didn't matter. She could, and would, say only what she felt that she needed to, in order to lift the awful pall of self-recrimination she'd lived with far too long already.

Taking a quick, deep breath to steady herself Hannah looked up at Evan, smiled shyly, put her hand in his and stood silently, glass in hand.

In the living room, only one small lamp was lit atop a high chest. The glow it cast over the homey furnishings was soft and warm and inviting, making the space feel to her like a safe haven. Here the trembling of a hand or a flush of shame could easily go unnoticed as secrets of the heart were shared. And here, too, the shock and disappointment that might appear in another's eyes wouldn't gleam quite so hurtfully.

Hannah had intended to sit alone on one of the chairs, but Evan obviously had something else in mind. He led her to the sofa, sat in one corner of it, then gently tugged on her hand to pull her down beside him.

She settled onto the soft cushions somewhat reluctantly, shoulders straight, back rigid. She longed to lean against him, to savor the strength of his warm, solid body, yet she didn't want to seem weak. As if sensing her small attempt at retreat, Evan let go of her hand. Immediately she scooted away just a little to put a less vexing distance between them.

"It's not my intention to make you feel ill at ease,"

he said. "You do know that you don't have to tell me anything unless you really want to, don't you?"

"Yes, I know," Hannah murmured, twisting her wineglass in her hand and watching the play of light on the crystal.

"I'm just here as a kind of sounding board—the nonjudgmental kind."

"Nonjudgmental would be good."

Hannah glanced up at him with a slight smile, then quickly looked away again, the kindness she'd seen in his eyes almost breaking her heart. You got to know a person well living together and working together as she had with Evan Graham, even over a short period of time.

Hannah had yet to see or to sense anything about Evan that wasn't completely honorable, good-hearted, steady and true. Taking a chance on him was not only something she wanted to do, it was also something she needed to do if she ever hoped to be free of the past.

"I think you have a tendency to be a little too hard on yourself. But then, that's true of a lot of people," he assured her in a teasing tone that helped her to relax.

"You, too?"

She took a quick sip of wine to gain some much-needed Dutch courage, leaned back against the sofa cushions and looked at him curiously.

"Oh, yes, Hannah—me, too."

He smiled at her again and the last of her reserve finally melted away.

"I suppose I should start at the beginning," she said, focusing on her wineglass once more as she gathered her thoughts.

"Start wherever you feel most comfortable," he urged her gently.

"The beginning, then, because it was good between Stewart and me the first few years we were together."

"How did you meet him?" Evan asked, his interest evident though not overly intrusive.

"It was at a Christmas party given by Milly Hargrave and her husband, Lester, seven years ago. Milly is the third-grade teacher who's retiring at the end of the school year."

"Yes, I remember Essie Dietrich mentioning her name today."

"Milly was teaching fifth grade then and Lester was the head of the mathematics department at the university. Stewart was one of the assistant professors working with him. They hosted the party at their home—an open house, really—and we were both invited. It was only my second year teaching and also my first Christmas living alone here. My parents had died within a few months of each other the previous spring and summer, and I was feeling especially sad and lonely.

"Stewart and I happened to be the only single people at the party, so of course Milly and Lester made a point of introducing us. I can't say it was love at first sight for me." Hannah paused for a long moment, recalling that cold December Sunday afternoon. "But I did like him a lot and he seemed to like me, too."

"I can certainly understand why he did," Evan interjected encouragingly.

Hannah glanced at him and smiled appreciatively, then took another sip of her wine before continuing.

"We had our first official date on New Year's Eve and we were married the following June. Not a very long courtship, but we spent a lot of time together.

Stewart was very personable and very attentive. He was also smart and had a good sense of humor. He enjoyed his work and was financially responsible. He also stood up to his father when he openly disapproved of Stewart marrying me."

"Were you in love with Stewart by then?"

"Yes, I believe I was," Hannah admitted after only a moment's hesitation.

She wanted Evan to understand that she hadn't married Stewart James out of desperation. Nor had she settled for the first man who had shown an interest in her.

"We had a lot in common including mutual love and respect, and we had a very nice life here together. We both had work that we enjoyed and we both wanted children eventually. We were thrilled when I found out I was pregnant with Will and we were so happy after he was born.

"Stewart wanted me to stay home and be a full-time mom, and I was really glad that we could afford for me to do it. I was so busy and so happy, watching my child grow and change, taking care of the house and gardens and Stewart, too, that I didn't miss teaching at all. I had everything I'd ever wanted—a home and a family to love and care for."

Hannah paused again, tears stinging her eyes as she thought back to that time. She had been so sure then that she was living her dream. She'd had all that she wanted and needed in her life—a loving husband, a healthy child, a safe, secure place to call home.

"But that all changed?" Evan prodded quietly.

"Not all at once," Hannah replied. "And not even so that it was all that noticeable at first. Looking back, that's the only reason I have for allowing things to go so far before I finally had the courage to acknowledge that something was really wrong. Not with me as I'd been thinking, but with Stewart. But then, though, it was too late to help him."

"I'm sure you did the best you could under the circumstances. You did say that he was ill, didn't you? But unless he admitted that he had a problem, either physical or mental, and tried to do something about it himself, there would have only been so much that *you* could have done for him."

"I understand that now, but then..." Hannah sighed and shook her head. Again she swallowed a mouthful of wine and tried to marshal her thoughts into some semblance of order. "About the time we were getting ready to celebrate Will's second birthday, Stewart began to have a problem with...anger management.

"He would have a fit whenever he didn't get his way, not only at home but also at the university. He would be incredibly unreasonable about one thing or another, blow off steam by raging around like a mad bull, then apologize and seem to forget all about it. Anything from coming home to find me talking on the telephone with a friend to being excluded from a luncheon organized by a colleague could set him off.

"Things that had never bothered him in the past suddenly irritated him to a major degree, including the time I spent taking walks with Will or working in the garden. By the time Will was three years old, I'd pretty much cut myself off from my old friends and neighbors. I rarely left the house on my own and when I did, I made sure that Stewart knew exactly where I was going and when I'd be home again. At one point, I begged Stewart to please go with me to see a therapist.

He told me that I was the one who needed help because I was so selfish and demanding."

"And you believed him?" Evan asked, taking her empty wineglass from her hand and setting it on the table beside the sofa.

"Why wouldn't I?" she asked. "I didn't want to believe my marriage was failing. I thought if only I could be more understanding, more loving and supportive, he wouldn't always be so angry and so upset. But also, after he refused to see a therapist, I thought about divorce. I even mentioned it to Stewart during one of his calmer moments. He just looked at me and said, very quietly, that I was welcome to leave any time I wanted, but he'd never allow me to take Will, too.

"He spoke with such authority that I believed he might actually be able to find some way to keep me away from my son. So I told myself that since he'd never actually harmed Will or me physically I might as well stay with him rather than risk losing my son and maybe even my home. I had already learned to put up with his controlling nature and his verbal abuse, and there was no way I could ever let him be alone with Will."

"That's the classic behavior of an abuser," Evan pointed out. "He cut you off from family and friends, then he worked away at diminishing your self-esteem, and finally he threatened you with the one thing he knew you valued most—your relationship with your son."

"I realize all that now, but while it was happening…" Hannah rubbed at the single tear that had slid from the corner of her eye to trail down her cheek. "I made excuses for him because I just couldn't face the fact that the man I'd once loved and trusted had turned on me so…viciously. I kept asking myself what I could have done to make his feelings for me change so drastically. He was having headaches, too, bad headaches that sometimes lasted for hours, even a day or two. He blamed those on me and Will, too. We were too noisy, too intrusive, too demanding or disrespectful of his needs."

"Did he see a doctor about the headaches?"

"He'd always had a problem with migraines, especially when he was under a lot of stress. He had prescription medication that alleviated the worst of the pain, but he had to take more and more of the pills to get even a small amount of relief. I urged him to see a specialist, but he refused to do it. He was becoming more and more paranoid by then. He even accused me of trying to have him committed to an asylum. On a couple of occasions, he became physically threatening toward me, too. I knew I had to take Will with me and get out of there, but I was so afraid."

"He put you through hell, didn't he?" Evan asked, his anger evident in the tone of his voice.

"Yes…yes, he did," Hannah acknowledged. Digging a tissue out of her pocket, she blotted the tears from her eyes and blew her nose. "But he was ill by then, seriously ill, and apparently he had been for a long time. We just didn't know it."

"How did you finally find out if he refused to see a doctor?"

"He was meeting with the dean of the mathematics department, Lester Hargrave. From what I was told after the fact, Dean Hargrave had asked Stewart to take a voluntary leave of absence from his professorship at the university due to his problems with anger management. There had been numerous complaints from students and faculty members, but because Stewart had tenure, he had been given the benefit of the doubt for almost a year.

"Apparently, Stewart's response to Dean Hargrave was an enraged rebuttal of the accusations being made. He…he had a seizure, a very bad seizure, and had to be hospitalized. Tests were finally done and he was diagnosed with an inoperable brain tumor. According to the neurologist, the tumor had almost certainly been the cause of his violent headaches as well as his increasingly more violent rages."

Hannah paused again to gulp back a sob as she recalled that awful day just over a year ago. There had been the telephone call from Dean Hargrave advising her that Stewart had been taken to the hospital followed by the long drive into Boone with Will secured in his car seat. She'd had to wait almost forty-eight hours for the test results to be studied by the various doctors called into consultation. The final diagnosis had come almost as a relief.

She suffered an awful pang of guilt as she recalled those first moments when she'd realized that she was innocent of all the psychotic blame Stewart had heaped upon her. Seeming to sense her sudden shame, Evan put an arm around her shoulders.

"That had to be a terrible moment for you," he said, his voice soft and sympathetic.

"In more ways than you can imagine," Hannah admitted. "I finally understood *why* he'd changed so much from the kind and loving man I married. But I also had to face the fact that he was dying as a result of the tumor that had caused those very same changes."

"How much longer did he live?"

"Only a couple of months," Hannah replied, dabbing at the tears in her eyes once again as she finally allowed herself to relax in the comfort of Evan's strong, warm embrace. "He was able to come home from the hospital for most of that time. He had to be heavily medicated, of course, mainly to control the pain. I cared for him with the help of a team of hospice nurses. They were wonderful, especially with Will. They helped me so much, and they were both here with us the day Stewart died. I would have been alone without them because I'd lost touch with all of my friends."

"What about Stewart's father? Didn't he offer to help you?"

Hannah noted the small thread of anger woven around Evan's bluntly put question, but knew, instinctively, that it wasn't directed her way.

"I didn't tell him that Stewart was ill," she replied with just the slightest hint of apology in her voice. "We hadn't seen or heard from him since before we were married. He didn't even acknowledge the card I sent him when Will was born. After six years of silence, I wasn't sure if he cared anymore whether his son lived or died. But then, I was making the funeral arrangements after Stewart died and I decided to call him."

"How did he respond?"

"He didn't say anything to me when we talked by telephone, but he showed up here for the funeral. He didn't speak to me before the service, but afterward, at the cemetery, he approached me and Will. One of my neighbors was there with me and she took Will off, so at least he didn't hear the things Randall said to me."

"What things?" Evan prodded gently, though the anger she'd heard twice already was still in evidence.

"First he blamed me for Stewart's death," Hannah said, her own anger roiling as she remembered Randall James's brutal verbal attack. "He'd talked to Stewart's doctor who'd told him the tumor had been growing for at least two years before he had the seizure. Randall assumed that Stewart hadn't sought medical help sooner because I wouldn't let him. He accused me of forcing his son to live in a backwoods cabin and then letting him die so that I could collect the money from his life insurance policy.

"Nothing could have been further from the truth, but Randall wouldn't listen to anything I said. He just rode over my words, roaring like a mad bull. He reminded me so much of Stewart during the year before he died that I wanted to run and hide. But then, he threatened to take Will away from me. He said he could, and would, prove me to be an unfit mother. I had allowed myself to be frightened by Stewart, but I wasn't going to allow his father to frighten me, as well. I told him to stay away from me and to stay away from Will or I'd go to the police and have him arrested. He laughed in my face, but I haven't seen or heard from him since.

"It's been so long now that I'm hoping he's lost interest in us. But sometimes..." Hannah hesitated, trying, unsuccessfully, to gulp down another sob. "Sometimes I still feel afraid of him and what he might try to do. He really isn't a very nice man, at all."

Unable to hold back her tears any longer, Hannah wept quietly. She had told no one else about all she'd endured during the last two years of her marriage to

Stewart James. Nor had she ever revealed her deep and abiding fear that his father might one day make good on his threat to take Will away from her.

"He's not going to do anything to hurt you, Hannah. There's no way he can take Will away from you, either," Evan said, his voice gentle.

His arms tightened around her, holding her closer still, and she turned into his embrace trustingly, accepting the comfort he offered.

"But he's a wealthy, powerful man and he has wealthy, powerful friends," she insisted as she tried to wipe away her tears with her sodden, ragged tissue.

"He would have to prove you're an unfit mother and a danger to your son first. We both know you're neither one of those things. You never have been and you never will be."

Shifting a little, Evan grabbed a handful of fresh tissues from the box on the side table and pressed them into her hands. Hannah used them to blot up the last of her tears and blow her nose. Then she looked up at Evan, her fear not yet banished altogether.

"But it would be my word against his, wouldn't it?" she asked.

"Your word and the word of people like Essie Dietrich and the Hargraves who know you and obviously care about you, and *me*, too." He looked back at her with a tender yearning that stole her breath away. "I know you, too, Hannah, and I care about you…quite a lot. Believe me when I say that there's no way I'd ever allow a man like Randall James to threaten you and Will."

A surfeit of unexpected emotions brought a new measure of hope to Hannah's battered heart and sorrowful soul. She hadn't known Evan Graham for very long, but her trust in him and the promise he'd made to her was unquestioning and complete. He owed her nothing, yet he seemed not only willing, but also able to promise her everything she needed.

"You do know that, don't you?" he prompted her, smoothing a hand over the wisps of hair that had escaped from her braid.

"Yes…yes, I do," she acknowledged with a watery smile.

Instead of smiling back, Evan just looked at her, the intensity of his steady gaze deepening to a heart-stopping degree. Her smile faded as she reached up and touched his face with her fingertips. Silently, she questioned the flicker of desire she saw in his eyes even as her body responded with a quickening she couldn't—*wouldn't*—deny.

"Hannah," he murmured. Putting a hand over hers, he turned his head and pressed a hot kiss against her palm. "Sweet, lovely Hannah…."

She smiled again at his endearment and started to thank him for his kindness. But before she could say a word, Evan bent his head and kissed her with a new and fiercely possessive passion. Sighing softly in joyous and unconditional surrender, Hannah clung to him, her hands clutching the fabric of his shirt as if she'd never let him go, and kissed him back.

Her lips parting for him at the first tease of his tongue, she tasted his desire for long, breathless moments as his hands moved over her. Stroking her back, he urged her closer, then cupped her breasts with an insistence that had her gasping.

Despite the layers of clothing she wore, the rub of

his thumbs across her nipples stirred in her a long-forgotten pleasure. Deep in her womb a first shaft of primitive longing settled into a throbbing ache of need.

Moaning softly, she arched against Evan's touch, wanting more. Immediately he took his hands away and raised his head, his expression now one of apology.

"I'm sorry, Hannah. I want you so much, but I shouldn't have—"

She reached up and put her hand over his mouth, silencing him.

"I want you, too, Evan," she said, holding his gaze. "I want you to kiss me and touch me and make love to me."

Hannah couldn't remember ever being so honest about her needs and desires. But then, there had never been another time in her life when it had seemed so imperative to give voice to what she wanted. She could think of half a dozen reasons not to allow this new intimacy with Evan to go any further. How much did she really know about him, after all?

But then, what more did she need to know besides the fact that she trusted him implicitly with her well-being as well as Will's? She had only instinct upon which to fall back, but she was sure she'd have known by now if Evan Graham wasn't the man she believed him to be.

"Are you sure, Hannah? Are you *absolutely* sure?" Evan asked, his bright blue eyes probing hers with renewed intensity.

"Absolutely," she assured him, placing a soft encouraging, coaxing kiss on his sternly drawn mouth. "Absolutely, *positively*…."

Taking both of her hands in his, he stood slowly and pulled her to her feet.

"Would you like to come upstairs with me, then?" he asked, still gazing at her intently.

"*Like* doesn't even begin to describe how I'm feeling about that at the moment," she answered with the smallest hint of shyness. "*Love* to go upstairs with you would be a better way of putting it."

Finally Evan smiled at her and drew her close for a quick kiss filled with undeniable promise.

"Do you want to check on Will first?"

"That's a good idea," Hannah agreed, touched, yet again, by his consideration.

Together they walked down the hallway to her son's room and paused in the doorway. Will lay on his tummy, the blue-and-white patterned quilt tucked up around his shoulders, with Nellie stretched out beside him, snoring softly. Hannah smiled at the sight of boy and dog, both looking so peaceful and carefree. Beside her, Evan put an arm around her shoulders and held her close. Oddly enough, his gesture heightened even more her sense that Will was important to him, too.

"He's sound asleep and likely to stay that way until morning," she said, her voice barely above a whisper. "But if he needs me for any reason, I'll be able to hear him call out."

"That's good." Evan kissed the top her head, then moved his arm from her shoulders to take her by the hand again. "Ready, then?"

"Oh, yes. I'm ready," Hannah agreed without hesitation.

She was amazed at how lighthearted she felt. Now that she'd freed herself from the nightmarish memories that had weighted on her so oppressively for so long, she was eager to live life and to love again. And she could think of no better way to celebrate life then by making love with a man as capable of and as deserving of respect and trust as Evan Graham. She might have only known him for a few weeks in real time, but in her heart, in her very *soul,* she recognized him as the mate she had given up on ever finding.

Just inside the upstairs room, Evan reached out a hand and turned on the small lamp atop the dresser. The warm rays of light barely touched the shadows in the far corners, yet allowed them to see each other clearly. No hiding of emotion would be possible, but Hannah welcomed the revelations to come. She longed to give as well as receive, and she wanted there to be no doubt in Evan's mind that she intended to be with him, and only him, on the intimate journey ahead of them.

Still holding his hand, Hannah turned to face him, a little shy but not the least bit nervous. He looked down at her, his eyes twin mirrors of her own desire. Yet there was something about the grim set of his lips and the rigid line of his jaw that spoke of second thoughts—perhaps even the tempting wisdom of restraint.

She reached up with her free hand and touched his face with her fingertips, her slow, soft smile meant to banish all doubts with a siren's invitation. He wavered for one long moment and then capitulated with a low groan that made her heart sing.

"When you look at me like that, I can't think straight," he muttered.

"Then don't think at all," she advised, her smile widening into a sexy grin. "Tonight…just…do…."

"Hannah…are you sure?"

"I wouldn't be here with you otherwise."

He gazed at her another interminable moment, then finally lost the battle he'd been waging with himself. Bending his head at last, he claimed her mouth with another of his fierce, possessive kisses that stole her breath away.

Clinging to Evan, Hannah not only welcomed his kiss, but also responded to it with a fervor of her own. The flame of passion in her soul that she'd been so sure had burned out forever fired anew, licking at her femininity. Languid heat began to spread inside of her, melting into liquid warmth—the precursor of exquisite pleasure yet to come.

"Hannah…?" Again Evan spoke her name as he broke off their kiss, the barest question in his voice. "I want you so much…I need you so much."

"I need you, too, Evan," she replied, again tracing the hard line of his jaw with her fingertips.

The last of his hesitation seemed to drop away as he hugged her close. Moving back again, he touched the wisps of hair framing her face. Then, tentatively, he tugged at her braid.

"Can I let your hair loose?" he asked.

"Yes…yes, please," she replied.

Slowly, carefully, he removed the fabric-covered band she'd used to secure the end of her plait. Then he deftly, gently freed her long, dark hair until it rippled around her shoulders.

"Beautiful," her murmured, running his fingers through the wavy strands. "You're beautiful, Hannah James."

"You're not too bad yourself, Evan Graham."

She touched his face again, then took his hand in hers and tugged him toward the bed. He moved with her willingly and once there, she paused. Reaching up to the top button of her shirt, she began to work it free. But with a knowing grin, Evan brushed her hand away and took over the job himself. Left to her own devices, Hannah started on the buttons of *his* shirt, also grinning.

They teased back and forth, taking one intimate step, then another, in the dance of lovemaking, shedding their clothes and their inhibitions along the way. They touched and tasted, tentative at first, then more boldly as sighs and whispers and thistledown laughter signaled need met and new wants discovered.

Beneath her palms, lying flat against his chest, Evan's heart beat strong and steady as the brush and rub of his thumbs on her tender nipples tugged at her deepest desire. The hot, heavy throb of his masculinity, straining toward the deft grasp and reach of her roving hands only added to the aching pleasure he gave her with fingers that delved and probed and slicked hot and wet against her feminine core.

"Bed," he said at last, his voice a low, insistent growl.

He pulled back the quilt, lifted her and set her down gently all in one smooth movement. Her breaths coming short and fast, she reached for him, wanting more and more still of his hands, his mouth, and at last…at last, the sure, swift, ultimate possession for which he'd readied her so completely.

But he stepped back from the bed, taking her hands in his.

"I don't have anything—" she began, unable to hide her sudden dismay.

"I do."

He turned away and crossed to the dresser, opened a drawer and shut it again, then returned to her, a foil packet in his hand.

"Not that I've needed a condom in quite a while…" he teasingly said, finally slipping into the bed beside her.

"Nor have I," Hannah assured him, suppressing an understanding grin. "I'm just glad you were prepared."

"So am I, Hannah…so am I."

He held out his arms to her and she went to him willingly. For long moments, he simply held her close. Then he began to kiss her—a nibble on her mouth, another on the curve of her neck, making her sigh with delight. Then to her breast he showed more demanding attention, licking and biting and sucking until she arched under him with abandon.

Hannah wanted to beg him for release, yet she didn't want the exquisite pleasure to ever end. When his fingertips stroked again between her thighs, she shifted and strained against him until finally she could no longer hold back her plea.

"Now," she begged with a wanton abandon that she had never imagined she possessed. "Now, please, Evan…."

Easing away from her, Evan sheathed himself in a condom, then settled between her legs. He smoothed her hair away from her face and smiled at her. Then, holding her gaze, he slid an arm under her hips and lifted her into his first possessive thrust.

"Are you with me?" he asked in a gentle voice.

"Oh, yes…yes, Evan…."

Hannah cupped his face with her hands and pulled

him down, her mouth seeking, finding his for a kiss that deepened all the more their intimate joining. He thrust into her again and she arched to meet him, taking him into her very core with a muffled cry of delight. Together they moved with an ancient, erotic rhythm until finally Hannah convulsed in a shimmering rapture of sensations, whispering "Yes, yes, *yes...*" in a voice she barely recognized as her own.

Hanging on to Evan, her hands clutching his shoulders, she lifted herself into him, not wanting the pleasure to end. He thrust into her again, burying himself to the hilt, finding his own release and taking her with him as again her world exploded in an exhilaration that was both carnal and all-consuming.

For a long time they lay together, still and silent except for the panting rasp of their breathing, joined body and soul in a brilliant afterglow that knew neither time nor place, but only each other. Hannah had never had such a strong sense of being cherished in her life as she had lying there in Evan's arms—not even in her most intimate moments with her husband. She didn't want to let go of that feeling and the belief that came with it of all things finally being right and good in the universe.

"I'm going to move," Evan said at last.

Though still too soon for Hannah's liking, he eased the transition with a deep, gentle kiss, making plain his own reluctance to release her. Side by side, he pulled her close again, his arms around her a strong, safe harbor from the storms of her past.

"Are you okay?" he asked after a few moments, his tone revealing his true concern for her.

"More than okay," she assured him, shifting to press a lingering kiss along the line of his jaw.

He immediately bent his head and captured her mouth with his, starting again the ache of need inside her. Raising his head at last, he added a quick kiss to her forehead.

"Hold that thought," he murmured, then eased out of the bedcovers. "I'll be right back."

"Promise?" Hannah asked, eyeing him with a sleepy smile.

"Absolutely."

He smiled back, then crossed the room and disappeared through the bathroom doorway. Tucked into the warm cocoon of blankets and quilts, Hannah listened to the sound of water running in the washbasin. And waited with anticipation for Evan to return.

In the space of a few hours so much had changed for her that night all because of him. He had helped lay to rest the ghosts of her past and had given back to her the self she'd once thought she'd lost forever. And he had opened a door to the kind of happiness she'd never dreamed would be hers again.

She wouldn't have believed it to be possible a few weeks ago. But suddenly, anything seemed possible—especially happy ever after.

Chapter Twelve

Evan dried himself with a towel, trying, unsuccess-fully, to avoid looking at his image in the mirror above the sink. With only the smallest amount of light from the lamp atop the dresser reaching into the bathroom, his face was mostly in shadow. But what he could see of himself he didn't like very much at the moment.

He could cite any number of reasons why making love to Hannah James hadn't been a bad thing to do. Chief among them was the fact that he was more than half in love with her. True, too, she hadn't objected in any way to anything they'd done. But the honesty of his love, as well as her desire were undermined com-pletely by the lie he'd told to gain admittance to her home, and now, her heart.

How likely was it that she would have welcomed his

advances if she'd known that he'd shown up on her doorstep at Randall James's behest? How trusting of his regard for her would she have been had she known that his services had been bought and paid for by the man she feared might take her son away from her?

Not very, he thought as he braced his hand on the cold porcelain sides of the sink and bent his head in shame.

Yet he had no real remorse for making love to Hannah. There had been nothing false, nothing even slightly untrue, in any word or deed he'd shared with her as they lay together in that narrow bed.

Given a second chance to do things differently under the same circumstances, Evan could honestly say he wouldn't. He might have insinuated himself into her life using a lie. But there was no lie in how he felt about her now—how he would feel about her from this day forward. She had opened a door for him onto hopes and dreams he had never dared to entertain in the past.

"Are you all right?" Hannah asked, the worry in her quiet voice shooting straight through his tormented soul.

Startled from his reverie, Evan turned and saw her standing just outside the bathroom doorway. She had wrapped up in one of the quilts from the bed and it flowed around her like a large, heavy cape. She looked as concerned as she'd sounded, and hesitant, too, as if she feared that she'd done something to upset him.

How to tell her that he was solely responsible for his misery? Impossible without revealing, as well, all of his shoddy secrets.

He wasn't ready yet to watch her desire turn into

disgust. So he reached out and touched her lovely face, offering her a reassuring smile.

"Yes, I'm all right," he said. "Really…all right…"

"Not even a little cold?"

She smiled back at him as he started toward her, and opened the quilt to him.

"Actually, I was just thinking that it's much warmer up here at night in bed than out."

He put his arms around her and drew her close, allowing the heat of her naked body to seep into him, heart and soul.

"Then by all means, come back to bed," she urged, wrapping the quilt around him.

"I can't think of anything I'd rather do."

Scooping Hannah off her feet and into his arms, Evan carried her back to bed. He left her alone there for the time it took to retrieve another condom from the dresser drawer. Then he crawled under the pile of covers with her and pulled her close again for a kiss that only began to express the renewed desire building inside him.

Hannah's response was everything he could have wanted and then some, her eagerly wooing him into tumescent need.

He would tell her the truth—he would find a way— a way that would help her to understand that he'd never meant her any harm—could never mean her any harm. But tonight…tonight—

"Wait," he growled as much to himself as to her, capturing her hands in his before she could tease him over the edge.

"But I want you again," she pouted prettily.

"And I want you, too. But first…"

Still holding her hands in his, Evan eased slowly down her body, pressing hot, wet kisses along the way.

"First...?" she murmured in a soft, dreamy, pleasure-soaked voice.

"I want to kiss you here." He put his mouth on her belly and sucked delicately, making her shift and sigh.

"And here..."

He moved lower still and put his mouth on her again with teasing tenderness, then smiled at the wild cry she made as she lifted her hips to him in open, abandoned invitation.

Early Sunday morning, as the sky outside the windows began to brighten with the first hint of dawn, Hannah slipped from Evan's bed and gathered her clothes from the floor.

"I should go back to my room in case Will wakes up earlier than usual," she'd said while still curled close in his arms.

"Yes," Evan had agreed, though he didn't want to let her go.

He hadn't slept at all, but unlike other times when he'd tossed and turned through the interminable hours, this night had passed all too quickly. He had wanted to hold on to Hannah and the bond they'd forged together forever and always.

In the darkness anything had seemed possible. Daylight brought with it too many hard realities, chief among them the lie that stood in the way of his hope for their future together until he laid it bare.

Even then, there was no guarantee that Hannah would understand his motivation. Nor could he be sure that she would be able to see beyond the professional falsehood he'd created to the honest, forthright man he had always been and would always be in his personal, private life.

Holding her jeans and shirt in her arms, Hannah paused and turned back to him, the slightest suggestion of uncertainty evident in her dark-eyed gaze. In one smooth motion, Evan slid from the bed, closed the distance between them and drew her into his embrace.

She came to him willingly with a quiet sigh, then stood silently, her head against his chest.

"Just in case you're wondering, last night meant more to me than I can ever say," he said, holding her tight. "*You* mean more to me than I can say, Hannah James."

He felt her lips curve into a smile against his bare skin and his tension eased considerably. He needed for her to believe in the truth of what they'd shared during the night. Only with that basic faith in him instilled in her heart would he have a chance of counteracting the lies he'd had to tell her.

"You mean so much to me, too, Evan," she acknowledged. "I wish I didn't have to go, but I have to think of Will."

"I understand."

He hugged her close a moment longer, then reluctantly stepped back, put his hands on her shoulders and turned her toward the doorway.

"Breakfast at eight?" she asked, smiling back at him.

"I'll be there," he assured her.

"I'm counting on it," she said, then started down the staircase, her bare feet silent on the narrow wooden steps.

* * *

Blue skies and bright sunshine were the order of the day, a welcome change from the gray clouds and relentless rain of the past week. Hannah insisted that the garden prep was proceeding on schedule, then declared their need for another day off.

The ground was too wet for a hike up to the meadow they'd visited the previous weekend. So the three of them, along with Nellie, walked along the gravel road that took them to the next mountain ridge instead. Hannah pointed out the homes of her nearest neighbors, tucked into the woods at various intervals along the way. Without her direction, Evan realized he likely wouldn't have noticed them at all.

The road itself eventually turned into an overgrown, impassable track where an old logging camp had once been in operation. Distinctive scars remained where trees had been felled, but it also appeared that new growth had begun to take root.

"My parents were lucky," Hannah said. "They never had to sell off their trees or their land. I'm hoping I'll never have to do it, either."

"You're not in a money crunch, are you?" Evan asked. "Because I have some cash set aside—"

"Not at all, especially now that I'll be teaching again." She looked up at him and touched his arm. "Thanks for offering, though."

"You do know that I'd do anything for you, Hannah. Don't you?" he asked.

"Yes, I know, and the same is true of me for you."

There was only one thing Evan wanted from her—enough belief in him and his basic decency to understand why he'd had to lie to her to keep her safe. But he couldn't say that to her just yet. First he had to sever his ties with Randall James in such a way that the man wouldn't be tempted to go after Hannah and Will with someone else's unscrupulous help—not an easy task considering Randall's bullyboy personality.

Then Evan had to find a way to tell Hannah the truth about himself. Standing between her and her former father-in-law might continue to be necessary even after he confronted Randall. Unless she found it in her heart to forgive him, that would be a very difficult thing for him to do.

That night Hannah went upstairs with him again as naturally as if they had been lovers for a very long time. She hadn't braided her hair in the morning, and all day Evan had been tempted to tangle his hands in the long dark waves drifting around her shoulders. Finally alone with her, he could resist no longer as they paused beside the bed to strip off their clothes. Looking up at him, she seemed younger and more vulnerable than she had at any other time they'd been together.

"You know that I'd never, ever, intentionally do anything to hurt you," he said, gently tipping her head back so that she had no choice but to meet his searching gaze.

"Yes, I do," she replied. "You know the same is true for me, too, don't you?"

"I know."

"Can we make love now?" she asked with a shy smile.

"We can do anything you want to do, lovely lady," he assured her, smiling as well.

"Anything?"

She eyed him in a way that left no doubt in his mind that she was a woman, not a girl, and a sexy one, at that.

"Do you have something special in mind?"

Hannah took hold of his belt and worked at the buckle with surprisingly nimble fingers.

"Get naked and I'll show you," she said.

"Talk about an offer I can't refuse."

He grinned at her as he started working loose the buttons of his chambray shirt.

"Well, you *could…*" she demurred.

"But I'm not," he assured her.

Tumbling her onto the bed, Evan had both of them out of their clothes in record time. But then Hannah took control again with another of her sexy come-hither smiles.

She straddled him and took a condom from the box he'd moved to the nightstand. She didn't open it immediately, though. Instead she held it in her hand as she trailed little kisses down his chest and across his belly, her hair falling like a silken mantle over his bare skin.

Evan's breathing slowed and deepened as he focused on the exquisite sensations resulting from her loving ministrations. Then he stopped breathing altogether as she took him in her mouth with tender care.

Groaning low in his throat, he tangled his hands in her hair and felt her smile again. From somewhere far away he heard the rip of foil, then using her hands and mouth, she sheathed him with slow and maddening strokes.

Finally Evan could control himself no longer. Pulling her up, he rolled her onto her back and entered her with one smooth, hard, determined thrust. She dug in her heels and cried out, convulsing with sudden need as he delved into her deeper, then deeper still, urging him on until their passion had been well and truly spent.

"Stay with me," she whispered as he held her in a tight embrace. "Stay with me always."

"As long as you'll have me, Hannah. I'll stay with you as long as you'll have me," he vowed though he hardly dared to believe that it really would be forever.

After their breathing had a chance to slow, Hannah spoke again as she lay curled close in his arms, her voice soft and slightly hesitant in the darkness.

"I feel like I've known you forever in my heart. But there are so many things I don't know, small things really, that I want to know."

Evan's gut twisted with dread as he realized what she was asking of him, albeit in a roundabout way. He had told her only the barest essentials of a made-up story, a blend that included a few facts, but was mostly fiction to get himself in the door.

He hadn't planned on having to embellish it. But then he hadn't actually planned on a lot of things happening that already had. He didn't want to tell Hannah any more lies, though. Not unless he saw that he had no other choice.

"Like what?" he asked, mentally bracing himself for whatever she wanted to know.

"Have you always lived in Charlotte?"

An easy one, he thought, and one he could answer truthfully while also filling in a few blanks for her.

"All my life except for the years I was in the army. I signed up right out of high school, mostly to earn enough money so that I could eventually go to college, but also to get away from home. My father took off when I was a kid about Will's age and my mother...my mother had a drinking problem. She died shortly after I'd fulfilled my military obligation."

"I'm sorry," Hannah said.

"I was, too, but by then I'd also come to terms with the fact that I couldn't help her when she wasn't willing to help herself."

Evan paused and drew a breath, surprised that talking honestly about the woman who had given him life but little else could still hurt so much after so many years.

"I'm sure you did all you could for her," Hannah added.

"Yes, well, it wasn't enough."

"Did you go to college after your hitch in the army was up?"

"Yes, I did. Then I worked for the Charlotte police department for a few years."

"And then you went to work for a computer company?" she asked, sounding surprised.

"Yeah, well, I was always interested in computers and programming, and I worked with them at the PD. I thought I could do better financially working for a private company. Unfortunately, I didn't foresee a merger and a job layoff in the future."

"You and a lot of other people," Hannah acknowledged. "Did you ever think about going back to police work?"

"No, not at all. I was ready for a change in a new direction, not a return to something that hadn't been satisfying enough to keep me interested in the first place."

Most of what he was telling her was basically true, Evan reminded himself. Only the merger and layoff had been fabricated. Of course, he hadn't told her the private company was his own, either, and he wasn't actually a computer programmer but a private investigator. But he would—just as soon as he felt that he could.

"Have you ever been married?" Hannah asked.

"I've had a couple of long-term relationships, but no marriage and no children."

"Did you ever want to get married?"

"I thought I did once, but it didn't work out, and afterward I realized it was just as well. We were already going in different directions when we first met. We both worked long hours and we both had issues we weren't willing to work together to resolve."

How else to explain the fact that he'd never felt good enough for a woman that he'd eventually discovered was using him to pay her bills and act as his beard while she waited for the CEO of her company to finalize his divorce? With a grim twist of his lips, Evan remembered how humiliated he'd been when he'd found out the truth.

Then he caught himself thinking again of how Hannah would feel when he finally revealed the lies *he* had told *her*.

"I wish I could say that I'm sorry your relationship didn't work out, but then you wouldn't be here with me," Hannah admitted.

"For a lot of reasons I'm not saying I'm sorry, either, but especially because you and I wouldn't be together otherwise. I came here looking for one thing and I've found something else altogether—something I hadn't realized was missing from my life until I met you."

Evan couldn't have been more honest about his feelings for her if he'd tried. But he wasn't sure how much his declaration would mean to Hannah once he'd been completely truthful about himself and his original motive for showing up on her doorstep. Would she feel too betrayed to believe anything else he said? Only time would tell.

"I feel the same way about you, Evan," Hannah said, shifting to give him a quick kiss on the chin. "You have helped me make peace with the past and learn to like myself again."

"I'm glad I could be of service," he replied in a teasing tone, glad that she seemed to have turned her attention from his past to the togetherness they now shared in the present.

"You have no idea…."

She cuddled closer to him, her hand moving across his belly in an exploratory manner that had him smiling in the dark.

"Oh, I probably do, but if you'd like to make sure…"

Evan captured her roving hand in his and placed a lingering kiss on her palm.

"Yes?"

"You could always *show* me."

He rolled her onto her back again and nuzzled her neck, nipping lightly at her in a way that had her twisting under him greedily.

"Oh, yes. *Showing* you would probably be best…."

Evan put off checking his e-mail until after lunch on Monday. The weather was favorable again and it was too tempting to pretend that the only responsibility he had was to help Hannah finish weeding the last of the flower beds. He hadn't wanted to let go of the magical intimacy they'd shared over the weekend, and that was possible only by blocking out the problems he still had to deal with in the real world.

But each time Hannah spoke to him in her sweet voice or sent him a shy smile, his gut twisted with a startling mix of guilt and panic. He was living a fantasy and he was doing it on borrowed time. Better to do what he had to do, and say what he had to say, so that there would no longer be any lies between them.

The message Evan had been expecting from Mel was waiting in his e-mail in-box marked *Randall James—Urgent* in big bold letters. Taking a deep breath, Evan read the few short sentences.

The man insisted on talking to Evan in person before the end of the day or there would be hell of an unspecified kind to pay. Evan e-mailed back, advising Mel he'd handle the situation. Then he went downstairs in search of Hannah, and found her in the kitchen.

She seemed to sense immediately that he had a problem of some sort even though he tried not to reveal his grim mood in any obvious way. Turning to look at him from her place at the counter where she was putting together the ingredients for a casserole, she began to smile, then hesitated, a frown creasing her forehead.

"Is something wrong?" she asked, wiping her hands on a towel as she started toward him.

"I had an e-mail message from an…associate of mine. I need to take a little time off this afternoon to drive into Boone and…take care of some unexpected business."

"Do you have to go now? Not that it's a problem…" she assured him with a sympathetic smile.

"Unfortunately the matter can't wait, but I promise I won't be gone long." He reached out and touched her cheek. "We'll still be able to finish that last flower bed before dark."

"It's not really a big deal if we don't, so take as much time as you need." She stood on tiptoe and gave him a quick kiss on the lips. "Just promise you'll drive safely."

"I will." He caught her by the arms and pulled her close for a deeper, almost desperate kiss. "As long as you promise not to try to do too much while I'm gone."

"I promise."

"Can you think of anything you need from town?"

"Only you back home again," she said, her smile sliding into sexy.

Evan pulled her into his arms again, this time for a tight hug as the words *only you back home again* whispered their way into his soul. He had never wanted anything more than he now wanted to have the right to call this place his home. But he had yet to earn a true place in Hannah's heart and wasn't sure yet that he ever would.

"See you later," he said, finally letting her go.

He would deal with Randall James just as quickly and efficiently as he could. Then he would sit down with Hannah and tell her the whole truth, and nothing but the truth, once and for all. And if she didn't understand...if he'd already made it impossible for her to ever trust him again—then he'd find a way to deal with it simply because he would have no other choice.

"So let me get this straight, Graham. You're telling me you've taken two weeks to come to the conclusion that I don't have a case against that hillbilly woman who's keeping me away from my only grandchild?"

Randall James's voice roared loud enough and angry enough for Evan to hold his cell phone away from his ear. He had found a place to park the Jeep on a store lot just outside of Boone where he could make his call without the connection breaking up. Now he wished for a static interruption so that it would be impossible for him to have to continue listening to the man's tirade.

Evan had explained the facts of the matter to Randall twice already. But the man still didn't seem to understand, not to mention accept, that there was nothing he could legally do to take Will away from Hannah.

"That's right, Mr. James. There is no proof whatsoever that Hannah is a danger to her son in any way. I have seen for myself that she is a good and loving mother. She is also mentally and physically healthy, and more than capable of supporting herself and her child now as well as in the future."

"Oh, you saw that for yourself, did you, Graham? What else did you *see?* A little ass and some tits, maybe? You've been spending a lot of time with the bitch. Did she get to you the same way she got to my son?" Randall demanded in a voice that had shifted to a sly, downright nasty tone.

Evan had to clench his jaw and count slowly to ten to keep from totally losing control. To rise to Randall James's bait would only stir up the old bastard all the more. There was no telling what he might do if he thought Evan had taken Hannah's side for anything other than strictly professional reasons.

"I've had an opportunity to observe Mrs. James over

a two-week period in my capacity as a licensed private investigator hired by you, Mr. James. I have completed my investigation into your obviously false allegations that Mrs. James is an unfit mother and I am now reporting my findings to you as you requested. I will be sending you a full written report, as well, within the next ten days along with a check for any balance remaining of the retainer you paid me once my fees and expenses have been deducted.

"I'm sorry you're not happy with the results of my investigation, but since it was initiated with lies and deceit on your part, I don't see how you could have anticipated any other outcome."

"How dare you call me a liar—"

"I'm also advising you to leave her alone. Your apparent vendetta against Mrs. James is unfounded, and any further move you make to frighten or harass her, as well as any attempt on your part to take her son away from her, will probably blow up in your face, Mr. James," Evan advised the man in a voice shot with steel. "You've done enough damage to her already, not to mention to your own son."

"I'll do whatever I damn well please, Graham. Your advice don't mean diddly-squat to me. I'll have your license revoked."

Evan punched the appropriate button on his cell phone, effectively ending Randall James's bitter harangue. Trying to reason with the man any further would have been an exercise in futility.

There was nothing he could say or do to hurt Evan, and Evan intended to make good on his promise to keep an eye on Hannah. Just in case he couldn't be there to protect her himself, he'd hire someone to do it for him.

Having dealt as best he could with Randall James, Evan now had to face Hannah and tell her the truth. The sooner, the better, he knew for a fact. He couldn't allow her to continue to build up hopes and dreams for the future based on false beliefs about him. But knowing what he had to do and actually doing it were two very different matters.

If he had just a few more days with her, he thought, turning the key in the ignition, then steering the Jeep out of the parking lot—a few more days to let her know how much she meant to him. Then maybe she'd be better able to understand that his lie had never been intended to hurt her.

Unless, of course, she *had* been an unfit mother.

With a muttered curse, Evan headed down the highway, eager to get back to Hannah, yet reluctant, as well. He might be able to justify to himself withholding the truth from her another day or two. But after that…after that he would finally have to come clean with her.

Chapter Thirteen

The gorgeous springtime weather held out through Tuesday and again Wednesday, tempting Hannah to start planting the seedlings in the vegetable beds she and Evan had prepared. But memories of years past when a late freeze or even a snowstorm had come at the end of April had her hesitating. Such harsh weather would cause extensive damage to her young, tender plants if they were in the ground.

With the flower beds cleared of deadfall and debris, she decided instead to begin culling and dividing the perennials. It was a task she'd always enjoyed, but working closely with Evan made it even more fun.

He was eager to learn all she could teach him, and was soon able to recognize certain plants by their leaves alone. He also had a deft, careful touch, along with the patience necessary to handle the young plants without damaging them as he lifted them from the damp soil and clipped off the frayed roots before replanting.

Hannah had never considered how wonderful it would be to have a partner who not only shared her love of growing things, but also didn't seem to mind the intensive labor involved. Certainly her parents had worked together well, but she'd tried without success to interest Stewart in her gardens and given up on such a possibility for herself.

Evan, on the other hand, reaped obvious satisfaction from each achievement, large or small. Watching him survey the work they'd completed at the end of a day, a proud smile tugging at the corners of his mouth, Hannah couldn't help but experience a full measure of joy, as well.

For someone who had never tended a garden in his life, Evan took to it like a natural. Hannah knew how unusual such an affinity was, and thus saw it as a positive sign for the future she had finally begun to believe she might have with him.

Her hope that he'd stay with her beyond the summer was reinforced, as well, each night after they'd tucked Will into his bed and climbed the staircase to his room together. Their passion for each other sparked and flared anew with each kiss and tender caress. Hannah had no doubt that in those heated moments Evan wanted her and needed her with the same deep desire that she wanted and needed him.

And yet…

As she used her garden fork to loosen the soil around a clump of hostas that had become too crowded to thrive, she shot a lingering sidelong glance Evan's way. He was focused on the forget-me-nots in the next bed over from her and didn't seem to sense her scrutiny.

Though she couldn't say exactly why, she'd had the oddest feeling that since he'd returned from Boone late Monday afternoon something serious had been weighing on his mind. He hadn't said anything at all about the business that had taken him there, and respecting his right to privacy, Hannah hadn't asked him about it outright, either.

But he had seemed a little distracted that night, and then later, in bed, he had made love to her with an urgency that had left her not only breathlessly satiated, but also just a little bewildered. And for a long time afterward he'd held her as if he'd never be able to hold her again when to Hannah their life together seemed only to be just beginning.

She wished that she felt more comfortable simply asking Evan what, if anything, was worrying him. But their relationship was so new that she might very well be reading him all wrong.

What seemed to her like silent brooding could just as likely be his way of quietly, competently thinking through an idea on his own before presenting it to her for discussion.

"What?"

The teasing tone of Evan's voice startled Hannah into realizing that he'd caught her staring at him. She smiled sheepishly as she sat back on her heels and shook her head.

"Nothing…."

"You were eyeing me rather pensively just a moment ago. Am I being too rough with the forget-me-nots?"

"No, you aren't," she said. "In fact, you're actually being extremely gentle with the little devils."

"Do you want to take a break?"

Hannah looked at her watch and saw that it was almost three o'clock. Will had agreed to take a nap after lunch and she'd have to go in and wake him up soon. Otherwise bedtime later could end up turning out to be a most annoying hassle.

"Might as well," she agreed. "Let's get something to drink and sit on the porch swing for a few minutes."

Maybe, too, she could get Evan to tell her that she'd misread him completely and there was nothing bothering him at all, she added to herself as she stood and brushed the dirt off the knees of her jeans.

They had just settled on the porch swing, glasses of iced tea in hand, when the sound of tires crunching on the gravel drive made Hannah look up in surprise. She rarely had visitors, especially ones that hadn't called ahead first to make sure she'd be at home, and she surely would have noticed if the message light had been blinking on the answering machine.

"Are you expecting anyone?" Evan asked, frowning as he set his glass of tea on the porch floor, then stood and started down the steps. "Essie Dietrich, maybe?"

"No, not Essie. I'm meeting with her tomorrow afternoon at the elementary school."

Hannah, too, set aside her glass and walked down the porch steps, pausing next to Evan on the grassy verge at the top of the drive. She was only mildly curious about her visitor. But she sensed that Evan was watching the break in the trees where the drive curved and the vehicle would finally come into view with something more akin to apprehension.

She wondered briefly about his concern as he put a protective arm around her shoulders and drew her close to his side.

"Are *you* expecting anyone?"

She glanced up at him as a faint tickle of unease crept up her spine. Hadn't she just been thinking that maybe he had some sort of problem causing him concern? Could it possibly be that problem was now coming up her driveway?

Evan didn't answer her, but the line of his jaw tightened and his eyes narrowed dangerously as the sound of the approaching vehicle grew louder still. Turning to look down the drive again, Hannah saw a highly polished black town car, now filmed with gravel dust, slowly round the curve. She vaguely remembered seeing a similar car at the cemetery after Stewart's funeral, a car belonging to his father.

A clutch of fear grabbed at her gut as the car crunched to a stop and the back passenger door nearest them flew open. Evan's arm around her tightened even more for just an instant as Randall James stepped out of the car and strode toward them furiously.

"Let me handle this," he muttered under his breath as he let go of her and moved forward to meet the man halfway.

Much as Hannah wanted to leap forward and boldly order her former father-in-law off her property, she actually found herself taking a cowardly step back. She was more than happy to let Evan face off with the angry, red-faced, heavyset man, dressed in suit pants and a rumpled white shirt, charging toward them like a raging bull.

"So, I was right all along, Graham," Randall roared, halting only a few paces from Evan and jabbing a finger in the air, almost but not quite poking him in the chest. "I pay you good money to get my grandson away from that woman and you're too damn busy getting a taste of her to do your job. I knew she was unfit to raise the boy and seeing you draped all over each other is all the proof I need. How long did it take you to tumble the slut into bed—a couple of hours, maybe a couple of days—and all the while on *my* nickel?"

Hannah heard what Randall James was saying— heard him loud and clear. But it took her several long frightening moments to fully understand the exact meaning behind his coarsely stated words. In fact, she was initially more concerned about the possibility of the old man taking a swing at Evan, and Evan taking a swing back, than in the words Randall spewed.

But Evan just stood there silently, a grim look on his face, waiting for Randall to wind down as he eventually did. Then very calmly, yet quite forcefully, he took the old man by the arm and almost roughly turned him to face the open car door. In a steely voice that brooked no argument—a voice Hannah had never heard Evan use before—he then addressed Randall, his manner cold and detached yet imminently authoritative.

"We discussed this matter on Monday, Mr. James. At that time I explained to you that Mrs. James never has been and never will be a danger to her son. Coming onto her property uninvited and spewing invectives is, to my way of thinking, very troubling, indeed. I suggest you get back in your car and leave immediately or I'll be forced to call the police and have you arrested."

"Why you arrogant—"

"Mr. James, get in your car and get out of here *now* or I will have you arrested," Evan said, cutting him off even more forcefully.

Though Randall sputtered with indignant, impotent rage, he finally did as Evan ordered, slamming the car door with violent force. Then his driver turned the town car around on the narrow drive and slowly headed back the way he'd come.

Only when the car had disappeared around the curve and Evan had turned to look at her did Hannah's whirling thoughts come together. The shape they took was at once ugly and unbearably, unbelievably painful as she gazed back at him, still too stunned to speak.

"Hannah, please, I can explain," Evan began, taking a single step toward her. "I can only imagine what you must be thinking, but I can also assure you that most of what Randall James just said isn't true."

The quiet voice he used coupled with the reasonable words he spoke should have soothed her. But Hannah's sense of betrayal was too great to be so easily shifted aside.

She put up a hand, palm out, to stop Evan coming any closer to her. Though she was shaking inside with outrage, she was amazed by the steadiness of her gesture, and then a moment later, by her voice, as well.

"So Stewart's father wasn't lying completely when he said that he'd paid you to come here and take Will away from me?" she asked.

"Randall James hired me to determine whether you

were a danger to his grandson. He accused you of being an unfit mother. He also told me you were raising your child in an unsuitable environment under deplorable conditions," Evan answered her, his tone matter-of-fact. "I was fairly certain that his accusations were false after I'd first talked to you in person, but I felt I had a duty to be absolutely sure about it—a duty to Will, actually. The only way I could ascertain that your son was safe with you here was to spend a little time with the two of you and that meant hiring on to work with you as a gardener."

"I take it you're not an out-of-work computer programmer, then." Crossing her arms over her chest defensively, Hannah tipped her chin in challenge. "In fact, I'm guessing you're not a lot of things I thought you were."

How many lies had he told her in the past two and a half weeks? Dozens, she imagined, and she'd believed every one of them like a gullible fool. She had been so willing to see only what she wanted to see— a good and decent man, down on his luck, who needed her as much as she needed him—that she had gladly allowed him to insinuate himself into her life.

He must have had a laugh or two at how easy she'd made it for him to do his job.

"I'm a private investigator. I own a small company in Charlotte that specializes in cases involving children." Evan, too, shifted his stance, as if bracing himself for her reproach. To his credit, though, he continued to meet her gaze head-on, and there was no hint of equivocation in his voice. "Everything else I've told you about myself if true. I've always lived in Charlotte, I served a hitch in the army, I was an officer on the Charlotte police force before I began working as a private investigator. I saw a lot of children living in situations similar to mine when I was a kid and I wanted to do more for them than I could as a civil servant."

"Like take a little boy away from his loving mother on the say-so of a wealthy, domineering, hateful, but basically clueless, old man?" Hannah demanded, allowing herself the brief pleasure of sarcasm.

"Not all mothers or fathers love and care for their children the way you love and care for Will. Once I'd spent a little time with you and gathered the information I needed, there was never any question in my mind that you were a danger to your son. I don't personally remove a child from a home, either. Not unless I see that there's an immediate physical threat to the child. I contact local law enforcement and children's protection services. None of that was necessary in your case."

"Why didn't you just gather your information and go? Why did you stay here and keep pretending…keep pretending that you—?"

For the first time since she had started quizzing Evan, Hannah's voice quavered. The painful realization of how completely he had deceived her grabbed at her heart and twisted with agonizing expertise. She had trusted him—*trusted* him to her very core.

Evan tried again to close the distance between them, but Hannah took a quick step back and shook her head warningly. He halted in midstride and put up his hands, signaling his reluctant surrender to her unspoken wish that he say away.

"The day I told you I had to go to Charlotte on business I actually drove to Asheville to meet with your fa-

ther-in-law. I told him then that I had no proof to sub-
stantiate his allegations against you. He insisted that I
hadn't looked hard enough and that if I couldn't get the
job done, he would find somebody who could.

"I thought at the time there was a definite possibility that he'd send somebody out here to cause you
trouble—somebody willing to do anything for the
money he could pay. I asked him to give me a little
more time to finalize my investigation. I thought I'd be
able to look out for you and Will that way, and I'd also
be able to keep Randall in check. I couldn't just leave
you here alone with all the work you'd hired me to do,
either."

"So you were going to keep up the pretense of being
Evan Graham, gardener for hire, indefinitely?" she
challenged him, again with a sarcastic edge to her
voice. "How altruistic of you."

"I wanted to tell you the truth, Hannah. Especially
after I talked to Randall again on Monday afternoon,"
Evan answered her quietly, finally having the grace
to look not only uncomfortable, but also obviously
ashamed of himself. "I swore to myself that I'd tell you
everything, but I kept thinking about how upset you
were going to be, and I just kept putting it off. Believe
me, I didn't intend for you to find out the truth about
me the way you did."

"Oh, I'm sure you didn't, but I have, and saying that
I'm *upset* doesn't even begin to describe how I'm feeling right now. You lied to me to get into my house—into
my life—into my *heart*. You took advantage of me in the
most hurtful way possible." Hannah straightened her
shoulders and eyed him through a shimmer of sudden
tears. "I think you'd better leave, Evan. I think you'd bet-

ter leave right now and never, *ever,* come back here again."

Giving him a wide berth, she strode past him, ran up the porch steps, then into the house. Only a few seconds behind her, Evan followed wordlessly. She had made it only halfway across the living room when the firm grip of his hand on her arm halted her in midflight.

"Wait, Hannah, please wait." Turning her so that she faced him again, he refused to allow her to shrug off his hold on her. "I didn't lie about my feelings for you just to have sex with you. I would have never done that. You mean so much to me. You have to believe—"

"I *can't* believe you, Evan. Don't you see that?" she shot back at him, her voice harsh, her breathing ragged. "The fact that you lied to me at the very beginning, then maintained that lie long past the time it was necessary, makes it impossible. All I can do right now is wonder how much of what you've said and done over the past few weeks, including making love to me, was real and true, and how much was just a part of the lie you felt you had to tell me in order to do your job."

Again Hannah tried to pull her arm free, but still Evan held tight to her. She was crying now, her face wet with tears that she brushed at futilely with one hand.

"Hannah, *please*—" Evan said again.

"I can't," she said, her tone sailing up a wild octave as she struggled with him now, desperate to get away. "I *won't*—"

"Mommy, *Mommy,* what's wrong?"

Hannah froze instantly, as did Evan, as Will's frightened voice echoed all around them. Mere seconds later, Evan released her, took a step back and shoved his hands in the back pockets of his jeans. The intensity of his expression smoothed almost instantly into benign as his gaze traveled past her to her son.

Finally free of his hold, Hannah turned to see her son standing in the living room doorway with the dog huddled close beside him. He was clutching Nellie's collar and looking at Hannah with wide, frightened eyes.

Quickly Hannah wiped away her tears with the palms of her hands, then crossed to him. Kneeling on the floor in front of him, she gathered him into her arms and hugged him close. For a long moment, he stood rigidly in her embrace, then he let go of Nellie's collar and clung to her, both arms wrapped securely around her neck.

"It's all right, sweetie. Everything is all right," she soothed softly. "Mr. Graham and I were…were disagreeing about…about something, but we're done now."

She hesitated a moment, then glanced back at Evan, silently pleading with him to confirm what she'd said. He met her gaze, his expression filled with profound apology.

"Yes, we're done now." He paused a long moment, still looking at her, a question in his eyes, then added quietly, "I'm thinking it would be best if I leave now… unless…?"

"Yes, that would definitely be best," Hannah replied, refusing to give herself a chance to have second thoughts.

She had made far too many foolish mistakes already, first with Stewart and now with Evan. She wasn't going to allow herself to be tempted into making yet another wrong decision because she was too cowardly to acknowledge the very real possibility that if Evan Graham had taken advantage of her once, he'd do it again given half a chance.

"I'll just go upstairs and collect my things, then."

Hannah stood, still holding Will close and without further comment headed in the opposite direction, moving toward the kitchen as Evan started up the staircase.

"Are you mad at Mr. Graham, Mommy?" Will asked, gazing up at her with more curiosity than fear after she'd settled him on one of the chairs.

Nellie, looking worried, had curled up under the table at his feet.

"Not mad, just…disappointed," she replied. "We had a disagreement about something he did, and we both thought it would be best if he left."

"Will he be coming back again?"

"No, he won't."

Will eyed her with obvious sadness for several long seconds.

"I really like him, Mommy. I'm going to miss him."

"Yes, well, I understand, Will. But sometimes when two people disagree about something it's hard for them to be together," she explained as carefully as she could.

"Are you going to miss him, too, Mommy?" her son asked, boyishly inquisitive.

"Yes," Hannah admitted, the urge to cry upon her once again. "Yes, I'm going to miss him, too, but some things can't be…can't be helped." She crossed to the pantry and retrieved the cookie tin, surreptitiously wiping away the fresh tears threatening to spill onto her cheeks. "Now, how about a chocolate chip cookie and glass of milk for your afternoon snack?"

"May I please have *two* cookies?"

"Yes, you may have *two* cookies," Hannah agreed, then spotted Evan lurking near the door leading out to the side porch, duffel bag and computer case in hand.

She halted halfway across the kitchen and met his gaze with as much determination as she could muster.

"Do you have everything?" she asked ever so politely.

"All of my belongings, yes," he replied, meeting her gaze, then added with a meaningful tip of his chin, "But not everything—at least not everything that I *need.*"

Hannah looked away as she continued to the kitchen counter, cookie tin in hand. She couldn't allow herself to be tempted to believe in him in any way, no matter how beseeching his expression.

"I owe you some money for the past three days. Let me write a check for you—"

"It's not necessary for you to pay me any additional money," Evan cut in. "The work I did for you here, especially the past few days, I did only because I wanted to."

"How magnanimous of you." Once again, Hannah had difficulty keeping her sarcasm under control. Setting the cookie tin on the counter, she turned to face him fully, adding, "But I'd just as soon pay you anyway. Then I won't be left feeling like I owe you…anything. In fact, paying you will give me just the sense of closure I need right now."

Evan looked as if he was about to say something more as she walked past him on her way to the bedroom to retrieve her checkbook. Something in the glance she shot his way seemed to stop him, though.

Then Will asked curiously, "Are you ever coming back to see us again, Mr. Graham?"

Hannah wanted to answer her son for him in the negative, as she'd done only a few minutes earlier, but she strode into the bedroom with silent determination. She was more anxious to get Evan out of her house than to quibble with whatever he chose to tell her son. She could set Will straight soon enough once Evan was gone.

Still, she couldn't help but hear Evan's response, more than likely because he made sure to speak clearly and distinctly.

"I'd like to do that very much, Will," he said. "But whether I can will depend on how your mom feels about it."

"Maybe when she's not mad at you anymore she would like it," Will replied with a child's innocence and enthusiasm. "I know I would."

"Yes, so would I."

"Do you think Mommy would mind if you gave me my cookies and milk now?"

"Probably not," he replied with the faintest hint of good humor.

As Hannah sat on the sofa and wrote out a check for Evan, then ripped it out of her checkbook, she had to blink back yet another prickle of unexpected tears.

How could a man who not only sounded so kind and considerate, but also *acted* that way at every opportunity, also lie to her so easily and so convincingly for over two weeks? More importantly, how could he then think that she would ever be able to believe anything he told her again? And if she couldn't believe in him, how could he even begin to imagine that she would ever want him to be a part of her life?

"Here you go, Will. Two chocolate chip cookies and a glass of milk, as requested," Evan said.

"Thank you, Mr. Graham."

"You're surely welcome, son."

Rounding the corner of the living room on her resolute march into the kitchen, Hannah saw Evan standing beside Will at the table. The expression on his face caused her to falter just a moment. Regret and something more—something akin to anguish—played over his features, giving her a moment's pause.

He had said that his own experience as a child had led him to the work he now did—work that involved protecting children from unfit parents. He had also said that he'd come to her house to be sure that Will was safe in her care.

He had admitted that he'd listened to Randall James's accusations against her, then followed up on them the best way he knew how. He couldn't have known she was a loving mother until he'd seen for himself the way she and Will interacted. That much Hannah could almost begin to understand.

But using her trust in him to lure her into bed so that she would willingly share with him the intimacy of making love while lies still stood between them was, to her continued way of thinking, simply unconscionable.

Slowly, Evan shifted his gaze to her and Hannah saw even more fully the torment he was suffering. Part of her longed to go to him and beg him to make everything all right between them once again. But another, more forceful, part of her clung to the strength of her original resolve as she moved forward, the check she'd written in her outstretched hand.

"Thank you for all of your help, Mr. Graham," she said, focusing on a spot just over his shoulder.

With obvious reluctance, Evan took the check from her, wordlessly folded it in half and tucked it into his shirt pocket. He retrieved his duffel bag and computer case from one of the kitchen chairs. But then, instead of walking to the door and letting himself out as she fully expected him to do, he hesitated, causing Hannah to brace herself for some sort of further onslaught against her hard-won better judgment.

"I'm thinking it's going to be difficult for you to find someone to help out with the rest of the work you need done in the gardens and greenhouses," he finally said in a bit of a rush. "I'd like to hire someone for you—totally at my expense. Someone who can come out here on a daily basis to give you a hand as needed."

Taken by surprise by his generous offer, Hannah wasn't sure at first what to say by way of a reply. After a few seconds, however, she straightened her shoulders and met Evan's clear-eyed gaze head-on.

"I appreciate your offer, but I'm perfectly capable of getting the work done on my own," she said with cool and quiet dignity. "In fact, after the experiences I've had with hired help the past few weeks, I'm more certain than I ever could have been before that I'm actually better off here on my own."

"Hannah, please, I don't like leaving you here alone—"

"There's no need for you to concern yourself about my well-being. I've been alone here for a very long time. I'm used to taking care of myself, as well as my son, and I'm certainly not afraid of a man like Randall

James. Stewart may have frightened me once, but all I feel for his father is pity."

"I still don't like the idea—" Evan began.

"It's not really your place to like or dislike anything I do, Mr. Graham," Hannah said, finally starting to lose patience with him.

"I'm finished with my cookies and milk, Mommy," Will said, scrambling down from his chair. Crossing the kitchen to join her, he slipped a small hand into hers. "Can I go out on the porch with Nellie now?"

"Good idea," Hannah replied, then shot a determined glance at Evan. "In fact, let me go with you. That way we can walk Mr. Graham to his Jeep and say goodbye to him."

"Okay, Mommy."

Seeming to realize that she wasn't going to back off her original stance no matter what angle he attempted to use, Evan met Hannah's gaze for one long, silent moment. Then he turned and led the way to the porch door.

She should have felt good about finally getting her way, but all Hannah really felt was sad. With a sudden, unexpected slice of perversity teasing at her wits, she also found herself more than half hoping he wouldn't actually climb into his Jeep and drive away, after all.

That was exactly what Evan did, though, his movements quick and efficient as he stowed his bags, settled behind the steering wheel and turned the key in the ignition. He didn't say anything more to her, nor did he look directly at her again. But when Will lifted his hand in a wave goodbye, Evan rolled down his window and waved in return just before the Jeep disappeared around the curve in the gravel drive.

That single simple gesture from man to boy had

Hannah's eyes filling with tears all over again. Angrily, she tried to dash them away with trembling fingertips, but she had little success. Beside her, Will tugged on her shirtsleeve with boyish concern.

"Don't worry, Mommy. Mr. Graham said he would come back to visit us as soon as you're not mad at him anymore."

"I know, Will, but thanks for reminding me," she replied, dredging up a smile for him.

"Does that mean it's going to be okay with you?" Will asked, smiling back at her.

"I'll have to think about it," she said, then made a deft attempt at changing the subject. "Right now, though, I'd better get back to work. Would you like to help me plant some flower seeds in peat pots for a while out in the greenhouse?"

"I'd like to do that a lot, Mommy," her son agreed, obviously happy to be of help doing something he enjoyed.

Hannah managed to keep Will, as well as herself, busy for the rest of the afternoon and evening. But eventually it was her son's bedtime, and after the requisite story and good-night kiss, Hannah was on her own in the all-too-quiet house.

There were any number of things she could have done—*should* have done. Of all those, she chose, of course, the one thing she quickly discovered that she *shouldn't* have done.

She climbed the staircase to the upstairs bedroom, determined to strip the bed and wash sheets, blankets and quilts—a kind of ritual cleansing she had somehow hoped would wipe Evan from her thoughts, as well.

His scent lingered in the bedding, though—his scent and hers still intermingled from their lovemaking the previous night. And when she breathed it in, a painful stab of loneliness unlike any she'd ever experienced lanced through her heart and soul.

She would leave the laundering of the bedclothes until another day, Hannah quickly decided, turning away from the bed. As she did, a piece of paper propped up on the desk caught her eye.

Even from a few feet away she could make out her name written across it in block lettering. She told herself to ignore it. There was nothing more she wanted to hear from Evan Graham. Yet she crossed to the desk, picked up the single folded sheet of paper, opened it and immediately read the simple words scrawled on it—once, and then again, more slowly.

Hannah...I don't have the time to say to you here all the things I need to. So I will say the one true thing in my heart. I love you too much to ever have intentionally done anything to hurt you or Will. Always believe that, if nothing else...Evan.

Hannah sank slowly onto the bed, the paper clutched in her hands. More than anything she wanted to believe that what he'd said in his note was true. In fact, a part of her *did* believe him—the foolish, trusting part of her that *wanted* to believe.

But in her head, rational thought warned that he had duped her once. Did she really want to risk being duped again, perhaps in an even more hurtful way? Because no matter what Evan had or hadn't *meant* to do, the fact remained that he'd broken her trust and he *had* hurt her deeply as a result.

Crumpling the paper into a ball, Hannah tossed it back on the desk. Then, with a renewed sense of determination, she turned back to the bed and set to work pulling quilts, blankets and sheets off the bed she had shared so passionately and so trustingly with a man she hadn't really known at all.

Chapter Fourteen

The intercom on Evan's desk buzzed insistently early Monday afternoon. Tipped back in his black leather chair, turned so that he could stare out the windows at the miserable rainy day holding downtown Charlotte hostage, he considered ignoring Mel's latest summons.

He wasn't in the mood to deal with anything or anybody—he hadn't been in the five days since he'd returned home.

Yeah, *home,* he thought, swiveling so that he could grab the handset on his telephone. The expensive, sparsely furnished apartment where he slept, or rather had *tried* to sleep the past few nights, was more than ever a kind of way station, even colder and more impersonal after the weeks he'd spent with Hannah and Will.

Better not to go *there* again, he warned himself.

"What?" he barked into the handset, suddenly welcoming Mel's interruption of his pity party.

Sensing his mood as any really good assistant would, and Mel was *really* good, she hesitated a very long moment, then offered an incredibly polite reply to his rudeness, shaming him rather effectively.

"I'm sorry to disturb you, Mr. Graham. I have Mick Stoba on line one. Would you like to talk to him now? Or shall I tell him you'll call back later in the day?"

Mick Stoba was the investigator Evan had assigned to keep an eye—a distant eye—on Hannah since Wednesday afternoon. His main duty was to park on the road to her house at night and make sure no one turned up her driveway, especially in the wee hours when no one would have any business there.

He usually had a gripe about something or someone. But he was quite capable of doing simple surveillance assignments.

"I'll talk to him now," Evan replied. "And Mel, I'm sorry I snapped at you a moment ago."

"No problem, boss. I know you have a lot on your mind right now," she said.

"Yeah, well, that's still no excuse for me to be rude to my number-one assistant."

"Just as long as you know it, I won't take any offense," she teased gently. "Oh, and in case you forgot, Mr. G., I happen to be your *only* assistant."

As Mel clicked off the intercom, Evan punched the button for line one on his telephone. He couldn't think what Mick would have to report at this time of day. He would have called in first thing in the morning had anything unusual happened the night before, and he wasn't due to start today's surveillance for at least another eight hours.

"Mick, what's going on up there?" Evan asked, curt and businesslike to cover an immediate rush of concern.

He didn't think Randall James would have the nerve to cause Hannah any further trouble. Not after the discussion Evan had had with him on Thursday in Randall's Asheville office.

But the old man had been in a bitter and vengeful mood for a long time, during which Hannah had been his chosen target.

"Nothing much, Mr. Graham," Mick replied with a yawn, sounding more than half asleep. "I just wanted to let you know I'm not going to have to keep an eye on that property I've been watching tonight. The weather forecast is calling for freezing rain and snow tonight into tomorrow. It's already colder than a witch's tit up here and there's sleet mixed with rain falling already. There ain't anybody in his right mind, including me, going to be driving up that damn mountain for the next forty-eight hours at least."

Evan's first instinct was to tell Mick to get his sorry ass up that mountain or find a job elsewhere. But then he realized that because of the man's griping, he'd also been advised, in a roundabout way, of something very important.

Not only would Hannah be isolated in her mountain home, perhaps for several days, but she also stood to lose at least some of the tender seedlings she'd set out on the deck just a few weeks ago to harden up. There was no way she'd be able to get them all inside the greenhouses before the worst of the snowstorm hit.

It had taken her an entire day to move all of the plants outdoors. But now she would have only a few hours at most before damage would be done. Only with a little help would she be able to save the plants she had already tended so carefully.

"Right, Mick, no problem," Evan said. "In fact, why don't you head back to Charlotte whenever you're ready? I won't be needing you for this particular job any longer."

"You sure about that, Mr. Graham?" Mick asked, suddenly sounding contrite.

"Yes, I'm sure. I'll talk to you again in a few days. Maybe I'll have something else for you then."

"Okay, fine."

Evan imagined the short, hefty man with beady eyes and a definite problem with body odor puzzling over his instructions, and couldn't help but smile. The next time he talked to Mick Stoba, Evan decided, maybe he would give him his walking papers as he'd been considering for a while now.

Granted, he appreciated the heads-up about the dangerous weather predicted to hit during the night. But he'd had about all he could take of the man's indolence and lack of enterprise.

Taking his suit coat from the hook behind his office door, Evan headed out to the reception area, pausing just long enough to tell Mel where he was going and why. She eyed him with momentary surprise, then nodded in apparent approval of his plan.

"Be careful out there," she instructed. "Let me know how it goes with Mrs. James, too."

"I will," he replied, then walked quickly to the bank of elevators that would take him down to the parking garage in the basement of the building where he'd parked his Jeep.

He hadn't unpacked his duffel bag since he'd returned to Charlotte. In fact, he hadn't even moved it from the backseat of the Jeep. His rain jacket and boots were there, as well. He had everything he'd need up on Hannah's mountain, including a change of warm, heavy work clothes.

She needed his help today whether she was willing to admit it or not, and he intended to be there for her. And maybe, while he was hauling peat pots from deck to greenhouse with her, he could also find a way to make her see that she needed him so many other ways, as well. Just as he needed her and Will….

South of Boone the roads were starting to get slick as the temperature dropped and tiny pellets of ice began to mix with the rain falling from the thick, gray, low-slung clouds hanging over the landscape. Forced to make the increasingly perilous drive more slowly than he would have liked, Evan cursed under his breath.

He imagined Hannah slogging back and forth on her own between deck and greenhouse, cold and wet and likely starting to tire. He wished he'd paid more attention to the weather forecast on the morning news. Then he would have been there with her already.

Evan saw the plume of wood smoke coming from the chimney of Hannah's house as he finally rounded the last curve in the gravel driveway. Lights glowed from the windows, too, but there was no sign of Nellie on the porch.

Evan grabbed his duffel bag, stuffed his boots and rain jacket inside it, climbed out of the Jeep, then cautiously made his way along the already-icy stone path that led to the back of the house. He spotted Hannah immediately, just as he'd expected he would, dressed in jeans and rain jacket, retrieving a handful of pots from the deck. Her hood obscured her face. But the downward slant of her shoulders gave away her weary resignation to what must have seemed to her to be ultimate defeat.

His heart filled with love and admiration for her valiant spirit, Evan called out to her as he continued forward, ignoring the rain soaking into his suit coat and the mud sticking to his leather loafers. He wanted to catch her before she headed off to the greenhouse.

"Hannah, wait."

She rounded on him, a startled look on her damp, pale face. She started to smile, then seemed to recall how they'd last parted.

Joining her on the deck, Evan saw her expression shift from welcome to wary hesitation.

"Evan…" She straightened her shoulders and met his gaze, seemingly oblivious to the icy sleet falling steadily upon them both. "What are you doing here?"

"I've come to help you move the seedlings. I heard about the weather forecast and I remembered what you'd told me about the danger of a late spring snowstorm—"

"I don't need your help," she cut in defensively. "I'm managing just fine here on my own."

"Now who's the one not being entirely truthful?" he challenged her with a knowing look. He waved a hand at all the dozens upon dozens of little pots still sitting on the deck. "You're not going to be able to move half of these plants into the greenhouse by yourself before they're coated with ice. The temperature is dropping too fast."

Hannah had the good grace to blush as she looked away.

"Maybe it's just that I don't *want* your help," she retorted.

"I've thought you were a lot of things the past few weeks, Hannah James—courageous, kind and loving among them. I never, until now, suspected that you could be childish, too."

In desperation, Evan had gone for broke, trying to make her see just how foolish her refusal of his help would be.

Noticeably stung by his harsh, but extremely honest, words, Hannah glared at him for a long, angry moment, making him think that maybe he'd gone too far.

"Suit yourself," she said at last, none too nicely. Then, eyeing his thoroughly drenched suit coat and pants and ruined leather loafers, she added with a sniff, "Although you're not exactly dressed for outdoor work."

He held up his duffel bag almost gleefully.

"I have everything I need in here. It will only take me a couple of minutes to change clothes."

"Whatever…."

Turning away, Hannah headed for the nearest greenhouse as Evan crossed the deck to the back door. There Will stood, along with Nellie, just inside the house, an avid look on his face.

"I heard your Jeep on the driveway, Mr. Graham," the boy said excitedly. Unlike his mother, he made no effort to hide his happy, welcoming smile. "But

Mommy told me I *had* to stay inside the house with Nellie no matter what."

"That's a very good idea. It's much too cold and wet out there for you."

"It's really icy, too. But Mommy said that maybe it would snow tonight. I hope so 'cause then we'll be able to build a snowman, won't we?"

"Yes, we certainly will," Evan agreed, ruffling Will's silky dark hair. "But right now I need to change clothes and go back outside to help your mom, okay?"

"Okay, Mr. Graham." Impulsively, the child grabbed his hand and gave it a tug. "I'm sure glad you came back. I really missed you and so did Mommy. She's been crying a lot, only she didn't want me to know so she said she had a cold."

"I really missed you and your mom, too, Will."

"Are you going to go away again?"

"Not if your mom will let me stay."

"I don't think she's mad at you anymore, just sad. So maybe she will," the boy suggested hopefully.

"Yes, maybe she will," Evan agreed, his own hope renewed.

He used Will's bedroom to change out of his city clothes and into a flannel shirt, wool sweater, jeans, heavy socks and his work boots. Then he donned his rain jacket along with the pair of waterproof gardening gloves still in one of the pockets and headed back out to the deck.

Hannah acknowledged his presence with the barest glance, which was about as much as Evan expected of her at that point. As long as she didn't flat-out run him off, he was happy. There would be time to talk later when all the seedlings were safely tucked away in the greenhouses.

The work was cold and wet and incredibly tedious. Care had to be taken on the slippery planks of the wood deck, so hurrying was out of the question. Despite all the bending and lifting and walking back and forth, it didn't take long for a damp chill to settle into Evan's bones, as well.

His fingers and toes ached, and after a while, he began to wonder if he'd ever feel warm again. But in the larger scheme of things, his discomfort mattered very little. He would have done almost anything for the chance to redeem himself in Hannah's eyes.

Evan urged her once late in the afternoon to go inside the house and let him finish on his own. She agreed only to take a short break to check on Will, then she was back on the deck again, much too soon for Evan's liking. She did, however, bring him a big, steaming mug of chicken noodle soup and a small thermos of equally hot, fresh coffee that revived him both physically and emotionally.

Apparently she must still care about him at least a little—although she shrugged off his thanks as if she hadn't done anything special for *anyone* she considered special.

The last of the seedlings had been safely stored in the far greenhouse just as night began to fall. By then, too, the sleet had turned to snow, falling steadily in a wonderland hush.

Evan and Hannah crossed the deck one last time on their way to the back door of the house, leaving tandem footprints in their wake. Behind them, the greenhouses glowed with light and warmth. Ahead of them, the house beckoned with its own snug and toasty promise.

Evan wondered if Hannah felt as numb as he did, then realized she must as she lowered the hood of her rain jacket. Her face was pale and drawn, wisps of her hair were crusted with melting particles of ice, and even after several tries, she couldn't seem to make her fingers, still in her gloves, work the zipper on her jacket.

"Here, let me do that for you," he said, tossing his own gloves onto the kitchen counter.

She looked as if she might protest, then seemed to think better of it. Lowering her hands to her sides, she gazed at him wearily as he dealt with the zipper, pulled off her gloves, then helped her out of her jacket. She was shivering noticeably, tiny tremors running through her body.

"Go take a hot shower," Evan ordered in a brook-no-argument tone of voice.

"But Will—"

Hannah gestured toward the living room where her son was more than likely quite happy watching television.

"Will is just fine, but you're not," Evan replied. "You need to get out of those wet jeans and boots and get yourself warmed up as soon as possible. You don't want to end up getting sick, do you?"

"No…but—"

"I can look after Will for the next thirty minutes."

"Then what?" Hannah asked with wide-eyed uncertainty.

"Then I'm going to take a hot shower and probably pass out from exhaustion on the bed upstairs. Unless, of course, you're planning to run me off again."

"Not tonight," she said, a quirky little smile peeking through her fatigue. "I'm not quite that bad an ogre."

"You're not an ogre at all. Now *go*."

Evan put his hands on Hannah's shoulders, intending only to turn her toward the living room and her bedroom beyond, down the hallway. But the tiny tease of her smile coupled with the way she looked up at him, all soft and feminine and…appealing, had him stealing a kiss that lingered long enough to melt a most heartening response from her in return.

In the space of a sigh, she relaxed in his arms and leaned against him, angling her head and opening her mouth to the first tentative thrust of his tongue. No fool at all, Evan took immediate advantage of the unanticipated moment, showing her the best way he knew how that their need for each other remained strong and deep.

"Yes, *go* would be good," she muttered, avoiding his gaze when he finally raised his head.

Stepping away from him, she turned and left the kitchen without a backward glance.

On his own, Evan smiled with masculine satisfaction. Perhaps all had not been lost, after all, he reasoned as he hung their jackets by the Franklin stove, then headed for Will's room, where he'd left his duffel bag, to exchange his cold, wet clothes and boots for a pair of warm, dry sweatpants and thick, heavy wool socks.

Just as he'd suspected, Will seemed more than happy with the entertainment provided by his electronic babysitter. Once Evan had changed clothes, though, he decided to enlist the boy's help in the kitchen.

"I thought maybe we could make dinner for your mom tonight," he said. "That is, if you'd like to give me a hand...."

"I'd like to do that a lot."

With a bright smile, Will jumped up to switch off the television of his own accord.

Together they scanned the contents of the refrigerator and, at Evan's suggestion, settled on fixing breakfast for dinner—an idea that had Will giggling with delight. He gladly stirred together eggs for an omelet while Evan put sausage patties in the oven, then chopped onions, peppers and tomatoes and grated some cheddar cheese.

By the time Hannah joined them in the kitchen, looking much refreshed to Evan's relief, the table had been set, there was bread in the toaster and the omelet was almost ready.

"Hey, you didn't have to do all this," she said, then slanted a wry glance Evan's way. "But in all honesty, I have to admit that I'm really, *really* glad you did."

"It was lots of fun, Mommy," Will assured her, beaming with boyish pride. "I helped, too. Didn't I, Mr. Graham?"

"You helped quite a bit," Evan acknowledged, then waved a hand at the table. "Have a seat, Mrs. James. Dinner is about to be served."

They ate mostly in silence, making short work of the deliciously hot meal as snowflakes tapped lightly against the windows.

"How did you know this was just what I'd want?" Hannah asked with a weary smile as she finally pushed aside her empty plate.

"I have to admit it was just a guess, but then, it was just what I wanted, too," Evan replied, returning her smile.

"Me, too," Will piped up as he carried his plate to the sink. "I love having breakfast for dinner."

"Well, then, I suppose we'll have to do it more often," Hannah said. "Now go get your pajamas on and choose a bedtime story, okay?"

"Okay, Mommy."

Evan stood, plate in hand, and reached for Hannah's, as well.

"No," she said, standing, too, and taking his plate from him. "You cooked. I'll take care of the cleanup. You're due a hot shower and an early night."

"I won't argue with that," he replied, his own weariness starting to take a heavier toll on him now that he also had a full stomach.

"I'm going to turn in once I get Will settled for the night," Hannah added, her gaze sliding away from his as she collected the rest of the tableware, then started toward the sink.

"Good idea," Evan agreed lightly, hoping to mask the sudden rush of disappointment that caught him in its grip.

Hannah had to be exhausted. *He* was exhausted. A good night's sleep would do them both a world of good, and in the morning...

Evan didn't want to think that far ahead just then. Better to simply believe that anything was possible—even a second chance at love with the woman to whom he'd already given his heart.

"Good night," she called after him as he started up the staircase, duffel bag in hand. "And...thanks...

thanks so much for all you did today and…tonight. Your help made all the difference…."

"You're welcome, Hannah," Evan acknowledged, then continued on with a quiet, wistful sigh.

The hot shower worked minor wonders on Evan's stiff, aching muscles and joints, chasing the last of the penetrating chill from his bones. He crawled into bed, sure that he'd be sound asleep as soon as his head hit the downy pillow.

Instead, he found himself staring at the ceiling, just barely visible thanks to the faint glow of light from the greenhouses filtering through the snow-dusted windows. His mind didn't seem to want to shut down, and the message it was sending to his body—putting all systems on high alert—had him shifting restlessly under the bedcovers.

The thought of Hannah, so close and yet so far away, tempted him with ideas best ignored. Yet the memory of how she'd responded to his kiss urged him to provoke a showdown between them *now.*

Why give her an opportunity to marshal arguments against him for tomorrow when she seemed so…amenable toward him tonight? Did he really want to risk the possibility that she'd run him off again, perhaps this time for good? Or did he want to make his case while she might actually be willing to listen to what he had to say?

Shifting on the mattress yet again and tossing aside the bedcovers, Evan sat up, determined, finally, to put thought into action. But then, the squeak of footsteps on the narrow staircase took the decision out of his hands in a most surprising manner.

A few excruciatingly long moments later, Hannah

appeared in the doorway, a dark and hesitant, but altogether welcome shadow. Like him, she was dressed in sweats and heavy socks.

"So you're awake, too," she said, pausing hesitantly, her voice barely above a whisper.

"Very much awake," he admitted.

"I…I need to talk to you," she continued after a few seconds, her voice wavering slightly, giving away her anxiety.

More than anything, Evan wanted to go to her and gather her close in his arms. Instead, he made himself stay put. Though she had taken control of the situation with admirable courage, her apprehension was almost palpable. By rushing her in any way, he could risk losing her forever.

"I was just thinking that I need to talk to you, too." He moved the bedcovers, making a place for her beside him, then patted the mattress. "Come and sit here," he urged her gently.

She hesitated so long that he thought he'd lost her. But then, she started toward him, and once again, hope began to sing its quiet melody in the depths of his soul.

Chapter Fifteen

Hannah padded slowly across the room, paused uncertainly beside the bed for several seconds, then sat down stiffly on the edge of the mattress, keeping as much distance between herself and Evan as she could.

Now that she was there with him, she couldn't think what had possessed her to seek him out in the middle of the night. She only knew that waiting until morning to sort out her thoughts and feelings had become more and more impossible for her to do as the hours had passed.

He had known how much she needed him that afternoon, and he had driven through rain and sleet without hesitation to be there for her. He had even ignored her angry attempt to send him away, refusing to listen to her false, and foolish, declaration that she could manage on her own. Without his help, she would have lost more than half of her seedlings, and she would have been the loser in so many other ways, as well.

For the umpteenth time that night, Hannah also remembered how Evan had kissed her earlier after all their work had been done. She hadn't even tried to resist the coaxing allure of his mouth on hers. Like an addict getting a taste of a desirable drug, she had succumbed to his ministrations without the least resistance.

Bad enough to turn to putty in his hands after the way he'd lied to her. But to come to him now as a supplicant made her question whether she had common sense left at all.

Much as she had realized that she'd be better off staying away from Evan Graham, though, in the still of the night knowing and doing had been two altogether different things. She had spent the days since she'd sent him away alternately applauding her courage and regretting her folly. For it had seemed, more and more, that judging Evan on the basis of one lie told for her son's well-being had been a big mistake.

Not to be deterred by her feeble attempt to keep her distance, Evan put an arm around her shoulders and drew her closer to his side. She resisted only an instant, and then just barely, before she leaned into his embrace with a quiet sigh.

How could she feel so safe with him if he wasn't really as good and kind and decent as she'd once believed him to be? How could she still want to trust him in ways that she had never trusted Stewart despite the fact that he'd been dishonest with her? Was it impulse or instinct that had brought her to him tonight? Did it even really matter anymore?

"I thought a lot abut what you said to me last week, and I…I understand a little better why you found it necessary to lie to me," she began at last. "I know you did it out of concern for Will, and I appreciate that—really, I do. Someone else might not have given me the benefit of the doubt. Someone else might have just taken him away from me. But it still…hurts…a lot that you lied to me for so long."

"It was never my intention to go on deceiving you, Hannah," Evan said. "My original plan was to investigate the situation here, make my report to Randall James, and if necessary, to the local authorities, and go back to Charlotte. I didn't count on falling in love with you in the meantime. I kept thinking that if I took a little time to *show* you how much I cared about you and Will, my actions would somehow negate the lie I had to tell to become a part of your life in the first place."

"But you knew that you were going to have to tell me the truth about yourself sometime, didn't you?" she asked, still not quite able to get past the fact that he'd perpetrated his lie for so long.

"Oh, yes, I knew that all too well. But I didn't know *how* to tell you in a way that you'd understand. Then Randall showed up here and took the matter out of my hands completely by revealing the basis of our unfortunate relationship. Considering how angry and vindictive he'd been toward you in the past, I should have known he wouldn't let you alone after just one warning. But I was so concerned about how to make things right between you and me that I stopped paying attention to everything else."

"I felt so betrayed that day," Hannah admitted, shifting in Evan's embrace to meet his gaze. In the faint light coming through the windows, his face looked haggard and sadness shadowed his eyes. "I wondered, too, if I could believe in anything else you'd said or done. I wanted to, but I just didn't know how. I'm not sure I do, even now."

"I swear to you, Hannah, only my reason for coming here was untrue. Some of what I told you about that—about looking for a change of pace and a change of place—actually turned out to be true, too. Being here with you and Will in this peaceful, happy place made me realize I'd found the missing piece in the puzzle that my life had become.

"I came here looking for the truth about you and along the way I uncovered some very important truths about myself. I also found the family I've always wanted but never felt quite worthy enough of having.

"I know that I let you down big-time by not coming clean as soon as I realized I wanted to stay here with you always. But I refuse to believe that I can't make things right between us now. I'm asking a lot of you, I know—to trust me one more time. I'll also understand if you don't think you can, especially if I've been wrong about *your* feelings for *me* the past couple of weeks. If you don't love me, Hannah, all you have to do is say so and I'll be gone from here first thing in the morning."

Her choice, Hannah thought as she continued to meet Evan's searching gaze. She could allow him to stay or she could tell him to go. Either way, she would then have to live with her decision because it was now hers, and hers alone, to make.

That she loved him was without question. He had found a place in her heart long before she'd made love with him. She had seen for herself his kind and gentle manner, his goodness and his decency toward her and Will.

He had already protected them and kept them safe from Randall James's threats. In fact, Hannah had no doubt that Evan would stand between them and any other harm, as well. She could trust him in that way. But could she trust him to be with her always in every way?

"Won't you be gone no matter what?" she asked, voicing her last, lingering concern. "You're not out of work. You don't need to live here with me and work in my gardens. You not only have a job that means a lot to you, but also a business to run in Charlotte."

"I've actually given that some thought the past few days," Evan admitted with a sheepish grin. "I don't see any reason why I can't run my business just as easily out of an office in Boone while still maintaining an office in Charlotte, too. As for not needing to live here or work here with you…Hannah, love, I've never needed, not to mention *wanted,* anything more."

Hannah looked away for a long silent moment, taking in all that Evan had said. She also remembered the words he'd written in the note he'd left for her the day she'd run him off.

The one true thing is that I love you, he'd said that awful day. And, she admitted as Evan put a tender hand to her face, urging her to meet his gaze again, his eyes beseeching, the one true thing was that she loved him, too. Loved him enough to also give him back her trust.

"You would do that for me? You would move your business to Boone?" she asked.

"For you, Hannah James, and for us, I would do that and more," Evan vowed. "Just tell me what you want, and I promise that I'll never let you down again."

"You, Evan…I want you, for now and always," she replied, her spirit soaring at last as she finally said the words aloud.

Evan eyed her for a long, exquisite moment more, then he smiled, slow and sexy, and *then* he gathered her close in his arms and tumbled her back on the bed.

"And I want you, Hannah…oh, how I want *you*…."

Epilogue

On a bright and sunny Saturday afternoon in mid-July, Evan stood under a rose-covered trellis in the midst of Hannah's flower garden. Standing with him under the trellis was Harvey Cox, the local Justice of the Peace. And seated in a small semicircle were friends and neighbors of Hannah's—now his friends and neighbors, as well—along with his staff, including Mel, to whom life in Boone seemed to be appealing more every day.

Unlike most days Evan had spent in the gardens lately, working among the masses of colorful blooms, he was dressed not in jeans and a chambray shirt, but a pale gray suit, crisp white shirt and sapphire-blue silk tie. And though his gaze was filled with a mix of pride and delight as he favored the yard with a last sweeping glance, his mood was mainly one of expectation as he looked again toward the house.

His life had changed in so many ways since that snowy day in April when Hannah had welcomed him into her life forever and always, and all the changes had been good.

An associate had taken over the running of his Charlotte office. Thus Evan's own move to Boone hadn't cost anyone his, or her, job. In fact, he had recently hired another investigator to work with him and Mel, so that he could spend more time helping Hannah harvest vegetables for her stall at the farmers' market and fill orders for her increasingly popular perennials.

Hannah's business was thriving, much to her surprise, but not his. The Web site he'd set up for her had brought in orders from all over the country just as he'd known it would. Evan couldn't have been more proud of her. Nor could he have been more proud to be a part of her life.

A sudden hush among the people seated around him made Evan's heart beat a little faster—that, and the sight of Hannah and Will walking slowly toward him down the garden path. She looked lovelier than ever to him, dressed as she was in a simple sleeveless ivory dress that skimmed her ankles. In her long, loose hair she wore a wreath of tiny blue forget-me-nots and in her arms she carried a bouquet of cupid's dart—papery blue, as well.

Beside her Will beamed proudly at the gathering of friends, then waved at Evan with boyish glee. A moment later, he ran ahead of Hannah, too excited to maintain her more moderate pace.

"Is today the day?" he asked, gazing up at Evan with wide, hopeful eyes.

"Yes, today's the day," Evan agreed.

"I'm so glad…Daddy."

"I'm so glad, too…Son."

Lifting the boy into his arms as Hannah paused beside them, Evan met her gaze. The smile she gave him, filled with love and trust, had his heart soaring.

"So glad," he repeated as he put an arm around her shoulder and drew her close. "So very, *very* glad…."

* * * * *

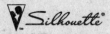

SPECIAL EDITION™

is proud to present a dynamic new voice
in romance, Jessica Bird, with the first of
her Moorehouse family trilogy.

BEAUTY AND THE
BLACK SHEEP

Available July 2005

The force of those eyes hit Frankie Moorehouse
like a gust of wind. But she quickly reminded
herself that she had dinner to get ready, a staff
(such as it was) to motivate, a busines to run.
She didn't have the luxury of staring into a
stranger's face.

Although, jeez, what a face it was.

And wasn't it just her luck that *he* was the chef
her restaurant desperately needed, and he was
staying the summer....

Where love comes alive™

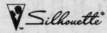

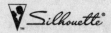

SPECIAL EDITION™

presents a new six-book continuity

MOST LIKELY TO...

Eleven students. One reunion.
And a secret that will change everyone's lives.

On sale July 2005

THE HOMECOMING HERO RETURNS

(SE #1694)

by bestselling author

Joan Elliott Pickart

Former college jock David Westport was convinced he
had it all—a beautiful wife, two wonderful kids and a good
business in his North End neighborhood. Sandra Westport
loved her husband dearly but was positive that he did
have one regret—letting her sudden pregnancy derail
his chances at a pro baseball career ten years ago. And
when a college professor revealed a secret that threw all
the good in David's life into shadow, Sandra feared her
marriage was over. Could David rebuild his shattered
dreams without losing the love of his life?

Don't miss this emotional story—only from Silhouette Books.

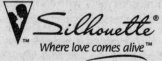

Where love comes alive™

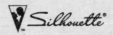
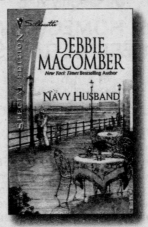

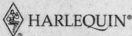 HARLEQUIN®

Ne_xt™

**Every Life
Has More Than
One Chapter.**

Receive $1.00 off

your Harlequin NEXT™ novel.

Four titles available each month,
beginning July 2005.

Coupon expires October 31, 2005.
Redeemable at participating retail outlets
in the U.S. only. Limit one coupon per customer.

RETAILER: Harlequin Enterprises Ltd. will pay the face value of this coupon plus 8 cents if submitted by customer for this product only. Any other use constitutes fraud. Coupon is nonassignable. Void if taxed, prohibited or restricted by law. Void if copied. Consumer must pay any government taxes. For reimbursement submit coupons and proof of sales to Harlequin Enterprises Ltd., P.O. Box 880478, El Paso, TX 88588-0478, U.S.A. Cash value 1/100 cents. Valid in the U.S. only. ® is a trademark owned and used by the trademark owner and/or its licensee.

OFFER 11171

5 65373 00076 2   (8100) 0 11171

HNSSECPNUS

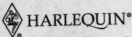

HARLEQUIN®

N͟e͟xt™

Every Life
Has More Than
One Chapter.

HNSSECPNCAN